ArtScroll Youth Series®

Rabbi Nosson Scherman / Rabbi Meir Zlotowitz

General Editors

Room

Published by

Mesorah Publications, ltd

210

A SUSPENSEFUL MYSTERY

BY N. BRAUN

FIRST EDITION
First Impression ... July 2004

Published and Distributed by
MESORAH PUBLICATIONS, LTD.
4401 Second Avenue / Brooklyn, N.Y 11232

Distributed in Europe by
LEHMANNS
Unit E, Viking Business Park
Rolling Mill Road NE32 3DP
Jarow, Tyne & Wear,
England

Distributed in Australia and New Zealand by
GOLDS WORLD OF JUDAICA
3-13 William Street
Balaclava, Melbourne 3183
Victoria Australia

Distributed in Israel by
SIFRIATI / A. GITLER BOOKS
6 Hayarkon Street
Bnei Brak 51127

Distributed in South Africa by
KOLLEL BOOKSHOP
Shop 8A Norwood Hypermarket
Norwood 2196, Johannesburg, South Africa

ARTSCROLL YOUTH SERIES®
ROOM 210
© *Copyright 2004, by* MESORAH PUBLICATIONS, Ltd.
4401 Second Avenue / Brooklyn, N.Y. 11232 / (718) 921-9000 / www.artscroll.com

ISBN:
1-57819-999-9 (hard cover)
1-57819-118-1 (paperback)

Typography by CompuScribe at ArtScroll Studios, Ltd.

Printed in the United States of America by Noble Book Press Corp.
Bound by Sefercraft, Quality Bookbinders, Ltd., Brooklyn N.Y. 11232

TABLE OF CONTENTS

In the Hospital

Bikurim Hospital, Jerusalem.

$\mathcal{D}$aniel Green looked out the window of room 210. How he longed to be outside, in the big world! The two and a half weeks he had spent in the children's ward, recovering from a bout of pneumonia, seemed to drag on forever. Sometimes his classmates Moshe Goldberg and Benny Klein would come after school. But the rest of the time, it was so lonely and boring....

A movement in the doorway caught his eye. In walked Nurse Anat.

"How are you today?" asked Nurse Anat, glancing at his chart.

"Fine, thank you. Do I have to take the pink medicine again?" he asked with a grimace. He hoped the answer would be no; the medicine tasted awful.

Nurse Anat smiled. "No. I just came to see how you're feeling."

She glanced around room 210 to make sure all was in order, and then walked briskly off to the next room.

"Good afternoon to all you wonderful children!" the beloved voice of Zalman Berger resounded through the corridor. Daniel looked forward to seeing the little old man with the short grey beard.

Zalman Berger

Mr. Berger, who had once been in the hospital for a long time himself, knew how boring it can be day in and day out. Now that he was retired from his job, he liked to come to the hospital to visit the patients and cheer them up. His favorite place was the children's ward. The childless widower treated the young patients as if they were his grandchildren. His pockets always held candy or pleasant surprises for them, and he would enthrall them with fascinating stories, the fruit of his life experience and fertile imagination.

At such times, Mr. Berger would say, "Listen carefully, and you'll understand how this invention works. It's very simple...."

At the sound of Mr. Berger's voice, Daniel would quickly jump out of bed and move the armchair closer so that Mr. Berger would be able to sit beside him.

Daniel was one of his most enthusiastic listeners. Occasionally, though, Daniel's attention would be diverted to the tip of Mr. Berger's long nose. Perched precariously on it was a crooked pair of glasses that sometimes looked as if they were just about to fall off.

Mr. Berger came in and sank into the arm-chair. "Ah, my dear Daniel!" he said warmly. "How are you today?"

Without waiting for an answer, Mr. Berger continued, "When I was little, I once saw two men soar into the air in a basket under a big balloon. All the townspeople ran into the field to see the flying marvel, and the two fliers waved hello.

Daniel Green

"As soon as I got home, I got to work building my own miniature balloon," Mr. Berger continued. "When it was ready, I decided to test it. I put our cat into the basket."

"Really?" exclaimed Daniel. "Did the balloon take off? Did the cat fly?"

"The truth is," replied Mr. Berger, "that the cat refused to fly. She jumped out of the basket promptly and ran away. I guess she didn't like the idea of being the first cat pilot."

Daniel smiled. The old man stood up, pinched Daniel's cheek, and headed for the next room.

Daniel went back to the window. The world outside looked so different from the third story of a hospital.

Daniel pressed his nose against the pane. In the busy street below, buses and cars moved in two directions. On the sidewalk, a young mother wheeled a baby carriage, a teenager stood at a public telephone booth, a few girls window shopped, a blind beggar sat on the street and held out his hand, a husband and wife hurried down the block, a gentleman with a dark hat got out of a white car....

Daniel sighed to himself. The world is so full of life, he thought. Everyone is busy going somewhere and doig something, while I'm stuck here in the hospital.

He returned to bed and opened a book.

A NEW FRIEND

*T*he sound of a bed being wheeled along the corridor disturbed the silence. *They must be bringing a new child into the ward,* thought Daniel.

The noise came closer. An aide in a green uniform wheeled the bed into Daniel's room.

The aide pushed aside a small cabinet blocking his path and moved the bed into place beside the wall.

"You have a new neighbor," said the friendly aide.

Uri Segev

The newcomer was an eleven-year-old boy whose legs were in casts. One leg, in traction, was held high up by a metal frame.

"*Shalom,*" said Daniel. "My name is Daniel Green. I've been here for two and a half weeks, recovering from pneumonia."

It will be interesting getting to know a boy who wears a yarmulka, thought the newcomer. *This one seems very nice.*

"I'm Uri Segev," he introduced himself. "I was in a car accident."

"You must be in a lot of pain," said Daniel sympathetically.

"I'm better than I was at first," said Uri. "They give me painkillers, and I'm really okay."

"*Baruch Hashem*," Daniel whispered.

"The doctors say I'll have to be here a long time," said Uri. "It will be hard to be far away from home and friends."

"Where do you live?" asked Daniel.

"In Revivim," answered Uri.

"I never heard of it."

"Most people haven't."

For a long time the two were silent.

"Can I bring you something?" asked Daniel.

No answer was forthcoming from the bed next to the wall. Daniel

Benny Klein

glanced at Uri. He had fallen asleep, probably from the influence of the painkillers.

There was a hesitant knock. Then Moshe and Benny sailed into room 210 carrying a small package of candies and letters sent by Daniel's classmates.

"Welcome!" said Daniel. "I'm so happy to see you two." He glanced over at the next bed, and when he saw that Uri was awake, he said, "Meet my new roommate, Uri."

"*Shalom*, Uri," said the two boys, approaching his bed. "We wish you a speedy recovery."

Moshe Goldberg　　"Thanks," said Uri.

"Uri was in a car accident," Daniel told his friends. "He lives in a place called Revivim."

"Revivim?" said Benny. "Where's that?"

"It's on the coast," answered Uri, "next to the city of Hadera. Actually, it isn't a village or a city. It's an air force base."

"You live on an air force base?" The three friends looked at him wide-eyed.

"Yes," said Uri, smiling at the look on their faces. "My father was a pilot in the air force. A combat pilot."

"He *was*?" asked Moshe. "What does he do now?"

"My father was seriously wounded," Uri said softly. "He's confined to a wheelchair for good."

"I'm sorry," said Moshe. "I didn't mean to hurt you."

"It's okay," said Uri. "My father is very brave. He was wounded during an important operation. But that's a story by itself."

"Tell it to us," said Daniel.

Uri took a deep breath.

"Even though it was quite a while ago, I remember it well, as if it happened this morning."

SECRET MISSION

*M*ajor Giora Segev was sitting on the leather sofa in his living room, leafing through a magazine.

It was late. His wife and his son, Uri, were fast asleep. In the distance, the waves broke with a roar against the rocks on the coast. Closer by, the noise of crickets wafted in from the well-kept garden surrounding the Segev home.

The phone rang.

Segev lunged toward it. "Giora," said General Doron Lavi, commander of the base, "come to my office immediately."

"Yes, sir," Segev replied.

The distance between the Segev home and the general's office was short, and Segev walked quickly. Within minutes, he was standing at the office door.

He straightened his uniform and knocked.

The intercom buzzed. Segev pushed the door open.

Lavi's personal secretary was sitting at the desk chewing the end of his pencil. When he saw Segev, he pointed the pencil in the direction of Lavi's door.

"The General is waiting for you," he said. "Go right in."

Segev walked into the general's office and saluted.

Maps of various sizes and colors covered the walls of General Lavi's office. He was carefully studying a map spread out over his desk. From time to time, he underlined something with a sharp pencil.

Lavi motioned to an empty chair. "Have a seat. I'll be with you in a minute."

Segev sat down and waited tensely.

Finally Lavi turned to Segev. "I called you here tonight because of intelligence reports about suspicious activities north of Damascus."

Segev leaned forward with interest.

"In the course of the past few months," Lavi continued, "the Syrian Army has turned old warehouses into factories for the manufacture of missiles. They fenced in the entire area, and military vehicles are constantly going in and out."

He moved the map toward Segev. "The secret factories are located over here. As you see, the entire region is mountainous and covered with forests. The approach is very difficult.

"These factories pose a dangerous threat to the security of the State of Israel," said Lavi. "We must destroy them. Only a brave, skillful, experienced pilot can do it.

"Are you willing to undertake a mission that involves a high degree of personal risk?"

"I will do whatever I am asked to do," replied Segev without hesitation.

"Very well," said Lavi. "Fly into Syria and destroy the warehouses! Your plane will be equipped with powerful missiles to do the job. But the Syrian Army has sophisticated radar for detecting incoming planes. It will take all of your skill, in addition to our sophisticated radar-jamming devices, to avoid detection.

"You will be joined by Captain Yishai Friedman, whom you know as an outstanding navigator."

Segev knew Friedman well from previous missions together. Segev had sincere appreciation for the highly qualified, yarmulka-wearing navigator.

Lavi looked straight into Segev's eyes. "Any questions?"

"No, sir," said Segev. "I'm grateful for the trust you are placing in me."

"Get ready," said Lavi. "Operation White Eagle begins tomorrow at 1 a.m."

OPERATION WHITE EAGLE

12:50

*I*nside the cockpit of the F16, the pilot and navigator ran a final check of all systems and engines.

"Sir!" said Friedman. "I'm ready. The systems in my charge are all in order."

"Fine," said Segev.

"Sir, I request permission to say *tefillas haderech.*"

"Go right ahead," said Segev. "Our mission is dangerous and tricky. Pray with all your might, and may *Hashem* help us return safely."

Friedman took a small *siddur* out of his pocket and prayed fervently.

At precisely 1:00, the command tower gave the signal. A green light flashed on the control panel. With a might roar of the engines, the plane took off.

The village of Jublaya, north of Damascus, slept peacefully. From time to time a lone dog barked. Two soldiers, chatting quietly together, walked along the dirt paths.

At the edge of the village, the two turned toward an old, tumbledown house. They knocked on the door.

There was nothing old or tumbledown about the inside of the house. Sophisticated computers were stationed on either side of a large room. Facing them sat two soldiers, their eyes riveted to the screen.

Thick cables emerged from the house to the nearby forest, where they linked up to huge radar dishes that scanned the skies and reported all suspicious movements.

"*Ya*, Ahmed," said one of the soldiers. "We've come to replace you. Have you received any special orders?"

"No," replied Ahmed. "I'm going to sleep."

"Me, too," said Jamal. "I'm exhausted. Six hours is too long for one shift."

"There's no one to talk to," said Ahmed. "Try complaining to the commander, and you'll find yourself in military prison."

"Have a good night," said the two as they left.

The new soldiers, Osama and Mustafa, took their places facing the computer screens.

"Prepare to fire," Segev instructed Friedman.

Friedman pressed three buttons in succession. A green LED started to blink. The missiles were ready to fire.

A white dot appeared on Osama's screen. He jumped out of his seat and grabbed the phone that connected him directly to headquarters.

"Unidentified plane at position 34," he reported excitedly.

"Acknowledged," responded the voice on the other end of the line.

Inside the F16, the air-to-ground communication system came to life.

"This is the command tower of the Syrian Air Force. Identify yourselves immediately! I repeat, identify yourselves immediately!"

"They've spotted us," said Segev. "Don't respond. We have to maintain radio silence.

"Keep your eyes on the radar screen," he added. "It's going to warm up here very quickly."

"Identify yourselves immediately," came the warning again, "or else we'll shoot."

At the Syrian Air Force base, the phone rang. "Battery of anti-aircraft missiles, open fire immediately!" barked Colonel Abdallah Shahidi. "It's an Israeli plane. Shoot it down!"

Major Yusuf Hamdan, responsible for the missile battery, received the order. He went to the control panel, aimed according to the data received, and fired.

"We will arrive in thirty seconds," said Segev. "Then I'll give the order to shoot."

"They've spotted us!" cried Friedman, without taking his eyes off the screen. "A missile is coming straight toward us from the north!"

Segev calmly maneuvered the plane out of the missile's way.

Suddenly the target came into view: a few big old warehouses hidden in the valley between two mountains.

"I've located the target," said Segev. "Ten, nine, eight ... three, two, one, fire!"

Friedman shot two powerful missiles toward the target. A mighty blast shook the earth and lit up the black sky with blinding light.

"I'm diving toward the target again," said Segev. "Fire!"

Two more speeding missiles shimmered in the darkness of the night.

The warehouses went up in flames. "Mission accomplished," said Segev.

The Syrian air base sent up three fighter planes. They picked up speed and soon sighted the F16.

"Shoot her down!" came the command.

"We've got to get out of here fast," muttered Friedman, "or else —"

Before he could finish the sentence, the F16 was hit.

"Giora," cried Friedman, as the plane reeled, "are you okay?"

"I'm wounded," said Segev, writhing in pain. "I'm losing a lot of blood. But you must bail out. The plane is about to crash."

"What about you?" asked Friedman. "I won't leave you."

"I can't pull the release lever of the ejection seat," whispered Segev. "Save yourself—that's an order!"

"I'll release your ejection seat," said Friedman.

Friedman pulled forcefully on the lever of Segev's seat. The roof of the cockpit opened, and Segev hurtled up into the night sky.

Then Friedman pulled the lever of his own seat.

The first second, he felt like a bullet being shot out of a gun. After a few minutes, he slowed down. The parachute tied to his back opened, and he began floating downward.

Meanwhile, the F16 lost altitude and crashed into the side of the mountain. As Friedman watched from afar, it exploded in a huge ball of fire.

IN ENEMY TERRITORY

*F*riedman landed gently in a valley. He quickly scrambled to his feet. Then he rolled up the parachute and hid it in the bushes. Enemy soldiers would surely search for the downed pilots, and he did not want to leave them any clues to follow.

Then, with a heavy heart, he set out to find Segev. *Giora is lying somewhere nearby, wounded and bleeding,* thought Friedman. *His life is in danger. If he doesn't get help quickly, it will be too late.*

The navigator reached into his survival kit and took out a compass. A quick calculation showed him where Segev should have landed. Without delay, he ran in that direction.

The chopping noise of a helicopter stopped him dead in his tracks. The helicopter itself was almost invisible against the black sky. But the two columns of light that it projected were clear enough. The light swept the rough terrain, showing its trees, bushes, and boulders. *The search has begun,* thought Friedman.

He crouched in the bushes. The noise came close, very close, and so did the light. It was so bright he could see it through closed eyelids. Friedman's heart beat fast. Would they spot him through the bushes? He prayed as he had never prayed in his life.

Little by little, the noise and the light moved further away. The helicopter had passed him and was continuing its search.

Friedman let out a sigh of relief. He waited impatiently a few minutes longer. *Giora is losing blood,* he thought. *Every minute counts!*

As soon as he dared, he peeked out cautiously. The coast was clear. He stood up and ran, hoping it wasn't too late to save the wounded pilot.

In the place where he figured Segev had landed, Friedman stopped running. He took a small flashlight out of his survival kit and began looking for clues. Some white fabric fluttering on the ground caught his eye. A parachute! That meant Segev was nearby.

He found Segev lying unconscious on the ground. His back and legs were badly hurt, but he was still alive. "*Baruch Hashem,*" whispered Friedman.

It was a miracle that the helicopter hadn't found Segev, but the search would surely continue. There was no time to lose. Friedman gently picked up the wounded pilot and carried him toward the mountain.

At the foot of the mountain, Friedman found a cave. The stench indicated that it had served as a jackals' den. But to Friedman at this moment, it seemed like a five-star hotel.

He placed the wounded pilot gently on the floor of the cave, near the entrance, and began to treat his wounds. He tore the sleeve off his shirt and made a tourniquet to stop the bleeding. With a little water from his canteen, he wet Segev's face and massaged his temples until he began to come to.

He took the radio out of his survival kit and pulled the antenna up. "White Eagle here. I repeat, White Eagle here. We were shot down. One wounded. Come rescue immediately."

At Revivim, the command room picked up the broadcast. The radio technician immediately informed General Lavi.

"Find out their exact location," Lavi ordered. "Tell them I'm sending a rescue team immediately."

⚜

In the cave north of Damascus, Friedman sat beside Segev. He moistened the wounded man's lips and tried to give him a few drops of water to drink. Segev mumbled words of thanks.

Giora's condition is not good, thought Friedman. Please, *Hashem*, send the rescue team soon!

Suddenly, he heard the barking of a dog in the distance. The Syrians were searching for them with bloodhounds!

Friedman dragged Segev deep inside the cave. A strong stench assaulted his nostrils from the remnants of the jackals' meal.

Overcoming waves of nausea, Friedman gathered up the remnants of reeking food and threw them toward the entrance of the cave. Then he went back to Segev and covered both of them with some branches from a bush growing nearby.

⚜

Holding a leather leash, Mohammed Hijawi led the search party. "Friends," said Hijawi, "you'll be able to go back to sleep soon. Searching for downed Israeli pilots is child's play when you have a bloodhound like mine." He

patted the dog's head. "Those two dirty Jews don't stand a chance. They're as good as captured."

Hijawi was right. The bloodhound picked up the scent of the Israeli pilots.

Friedman listened carefully. Barks and the noise of army boots treading the uneven terrain broke the silence of the night. The sounds came closer... and closer.

The bloodhound led Hijawi and his search party straight to the entrance of the cave.

Friedman held his breath. "*Hashem*, make the dog fall for my trick!" he prayed fervently. "Save us from the Syrian search party!"

At the entrance of the cave, the dog stopped short.

Its keen sense of smell was thoroughly confused. The stench of the leftovers of the jackals' meal, which Friedman had thrown near the cave's entrance, overpowered the scent of the Israelis for whom the dog was searching.

The bloodhound sat down on its hind legs. Eventually its animal inclination overcame its long training, and it began to nibble at the bones.

"Just look at him, *ya* Mohammed!" teased one of the soldiers. "A whiff of the jackals' leftovers, and your dog that you boast about forgets its mission."

Hijawi, stung to the quick, pulled angrily at the leash and shouted to the bloodhound to continue the search.

The soldiers moved on.

Friedman and Segev continued to lie in their hiding place.

Suddenly the radio buzzed. "White Eagle, White Eagle, give your exact location."

"A cave at the foot of a mountain at number 33," replied Friedman. "Hurry! Medical help urgently needed."

"We'll be there in five minutes. Prepare for evacuation."

"Did you hear that, Giora?" said Friedman, bending over the wounded man. "They're coming to rescue us. Hold on just a little while longer."

The chopping of helicopter blades grew louder.

Friedman was not the only one who heard the noise. The Syrian search party also heard it.

"Catch the Israeli pilots!" ordered the Syrian commander. "Don't let them escape!"

A helicopter approached the cave. Leaving the engine running, three men jumped out. Together they picked up Segev and carried him into the helicopter. Friedman followed right behind.

Zing. A bullet whistled nearby, barely missing him.

A heavy machine-gun attached to the side of the helicopter returned fire. The search party scrambled for shelter behind rocks.

The helicopter lifted off, turned around, and headed back to Israel.

SUSPICION

"Wow!" said Daniel.

"Unbelievable!" said Benny.

"By the way," said Moshe, "what happened to the helicopter?"

"It arrived safely in Israel and took my father straight to the hospital," said Uri. "He had several operations, but the damage to his back couldn't be undone. Now he's confined to a wheel-chair for the rest of his life.

"But don't be sad," said Uri. "My father is very brave, and he tries to live as normally as possible. He insists on continuing to serve in the air force. Of course, he can't fly planes anymore. Now he's a teacher and advisor."

Moshe glanced at his watch. It was 6 o'clock, and they had to get home for supper.

"Come, Benny," said Moshe. "It's time to go."

"Just a minute," said Benny, who had been looking out the window. "Something strange is going on out there."

Moshe and Daniel came over and stood beside him.

"You see the blind beggar with dark glasses sitting on the ground?" asked Benny.

"Yes," they all answered. "What's unusual about him?"

"Did you notice the cane beside him?" Benny continued to inquire.

"So what?" said Moshe. "Many blind people have a cane to help them walk."

"That's just it," said Benny. "A minute ago, the blind beggar stood up and walked to the green bench. When he got there, he bent over the back of the bench and then returned to his place—all without the cane!"

"What did he do behind the bench?" asked Uri from his bed.

"I don't know," replied Benny. "Maybe he put something there, or took something from there. Now I can't see behind the bench because a man in a dark hat is sitting on it."

After a while, the man in the dark hat got into a white car and drove off.

"You know something?" said Daniel pensively. "I think I've seen that person somewhere before, but I can't remember where."

"You have a good imagination," joked Uri. "Besides, you're still under the influence of my story. You're getting carried away."

"Maybe you're right," muttered Daniel. "But then again, maybe you're not."

The next morning, Daniel went to the window from time to time. The folded cartons on which the blind beggar sat were there, but he himself had not yet arrived.

In the afternoon, Daniel suddenly saw the blind beggar walking up the street, feeling his way with his cane.

When he reached his usual place, the beggar sat down on the folded cartons and held out his hand, palm up, to passersby.

Daniel looked at his watch. It was 4 o'clock.

At precisely 6, the beggar stood up, went over to the green bench, and bent over. Daniel thought he saw him hide something behind the bench.

When the blind beggar finished, he returned to his place, took his cane and the bag containing his belongings, and left.

For a few long minutes, nothing happened.

Suddenly a white car drove up, and out stepped a distinguished looking gentleman in a dark hat.

Daniel held his breath.

It was the same man he had seen the day before!

"Something very strange is going on here," thought Daniel.

Uri was dozing. When he woke up, Daniel hurried to tell him what he had observed.

"Very strange indeed," Uri agreed. "Maybe it's just a string of coincidences, or maybe there really is more to it. Keep an eye out and see whether it happens again."

In the Goldberg residence, the telephone rang.

"Moshe," his mother called, "you have a phone call."

Moshe picked up the receiver and was surprised to hear Daniel's voice. "Moshe," he said, sounding very secretive, "can you come to the hospital tomorrow?"

"Sure," said Moshe. "What's up?"

"It's not something to talk about over the phone," said Daniel mysteriously. "Bring Benny with you."

"Sure," said Moshe. "We'll be there right after school."

"Oh," said Daniel, as if recalling something important, "get here before 5."

The next day...

"Children!" hollered the hospital guard. "Where are you running?"

"We came to visit a friend," answered Moshe and Benny. "He's in the children's ward."

"Okay," said the guard. "You may go in. But remember that this is a hospital, not a race track."

They found Daniel and Uri whispering excitedly.

"What's up?" asked Benny.

"Tell us already," said Moshe.

Daniel related what he had seen the evening before.

"Very strange indeed," confirmed Moshe.

"I would call it suspicious," added Benny.

"Do you think the same thing will happen again today?" asked Moshe, opening his eyes wide.

"That's exactly why I asked you to come," said Daniel. "If anything happens, we'll see it together."

Three noses pressed against the windowpane of room 210. Uri, confined to bed, received regular updates.

"It is now 5 to 6," said Daniel. "If I'm right, in exactly 5 minutes the blind beggar will stand up and go over to the bench."

To the astonishment of the three friends, that is exactly what happened.

At precisely 6 o'clock, the blind man stood up. Without taking the cane, he went over to the green bench and bent over the back.

"Did you see that?" whispered Daniel. "He hid something."

"Did you manage to see what it was?" asked Uri from his bed.

"It looked to me like a piece of paper," said Benny.

"Maybe he's eccentric," said Moshe, "and he likes to hide papers behind the public benches at a certain time. People have all kinds of idiosyncrasies."

"Just a minute," said Benny, turning to Daniel. "You told us that yesterday, after the beggar left, a man in a dark hat got out of a white car—the same man that we saw two days ago."

"Yes," Daniel confirmed.

"Then where's the white car?" asked Benny.

"I don't know," said Daniel.

"There he is!" cried Moshe suddenly.

"Who?" asked the friends.

"The man in the dark hat," said Moshe. "He's walking slowly up the block!"

The gentleman was strolling along at a relaxed pace. When he reached the bench, he sat down and closed his eyes, apparently to doze.

"Pay attention to each movement," whispered Daniel.

Suddenly, the man slowly extended his hand behind the bench, picked something up, and slipped it into his pocket. Then he stood up and walked away.

"Did you see that?" they all said excitedly. "The man in the dark hat picked up the paper that the beggar had hidden."

"What do we do now?" asked Uri. "This is really suspicious. Maybe we should report it to the police."

"And tell them what?" said Moshe. "That we saw a blind beggar hiding a piece of paper, and a distinguished gentleman putting the paper into his pocket? What crime is that?"

"Moshe is right," said Benny.

"So what should we do?" asked Uri.

"First of all," said Daniel, "all of us need to have a conference together."

The three gathered around Uri's bed and began to whisper.

YOUNG SLEUTHS IN ACTION

"In my opinion," said Uri, "we've come upon something big!"

"What is the blind beggar hiding behind the bench?" asked Benny.

"Maybe it's some message or information that he's trying to send," suggested Moshe.

"A message to the man in the dark hat," added Daniel.

"How can we know for sure?" asked Uri.

"There's only one way," said Daniel.

He paused. "We have to take the paper ourselves before the man in the dark hat comes for it."

"What?" The three friends looked at Daniel in astonishment.

"You would need tremendous courage to do such a thing," said Uri.

"Indeed," Daniel agreed. "But maybe we can plan something simple."

"Like what, for instance?" asked Moshe.

Daniel, standing like a commander amidst his troops, began to unfold his plan.

"One of us will stand further down the street. When he sees the man in the dark hat come by, he will detain him for a few seconds.

"Another one of us," continued Daniel, "will sit on the green bench. The beggar will come and hide the paper. When he turns around to go back, that second boy will find the paper and then slip away quickly."

"Who will carry out the mission?" asked Moshe.

"I would love to participate," said Uri, "but unfortunately, as you know, I'm stuck in bed with my leg in traction."

"And I'm not allowed out of the hospital," said Daniel.

"That leaves Moshe and me," observed Benny.

"You, Benny, have good, quick hands," continued Daniel. "We need you to find the paper."

"I guess I volunteer to detain the gentleman in the dark hat," said Moshe. A chill crept up his spine.

"I have a question," said Benny. "Why do I have to wait for the beggar to turn his back? He can't see me anyway!"

"Are you sure he's blind?" asked Daniel.

At recess the next day, Moshe and Benny didn't join the ball game. They stood on the side whispering together.

"Do you think our plan is safe?" asked Moshe nervously. "It sounds a little dangerous to me."

"I don't know," said Benny. "But what else can we do? Go to the police?"

"We've already discussed that," said Moshe. "We have nothing but vague suspicions. They'll laugh us out of the police station."

"That's why," said Benny thoughtfully, "it might be our duty to learn more about these strange events. If we find any concrete evidence, we'll give all the information to the police."

"Is our decision final, then?" asked Moshe hesitantly.

"Our decision is final," Benny answered firmly.

5:20. Tension mounted in room 210. The three friends gathered around Uri's bed and held a whispered conference about the final details of the plan. From time to time, one of them went over to the window and looked out at the blind beggar. He was sitting in his usual place, oblivious to the excited preparations going on in the building facing him.

Moshe chewed his fingernails. He looked scared.

"Don't worry." Benny put a soothing hand on his shoulder. "It won't take long."

"I'm not worried," said Moshe. "Your mission is even more difficult than mine."

"*B'ezras Hashem*, everything will go just fine," said Benny confidently. "What could possibly happen?"

5:50.

"It's time," said Daniel. "Benny, go to the bench and take your place."

Benny put a book under his arm and went out.

From the window of room 210, the friends watched as Benny sat down on the bench, opened the book, and pretended to read.

"Now it's your turn," Daniel told Moshe. "Go stand there, near the streetlight."

Moshe went out to the street and began walking toward his position.

"What suspense!" said Uri from his bed. "I wish I could get up and watch from the window."

"Don't worry," Daniel consoled him. "I'll keep you posted."

At 6 o'clock sharp, the beggar stood up, went over to the green bench, tarried there a minute... and then stealthily bent down and hid something behind the bench.

He turned around and started back.

He returned to his place, picked up the plastic bag containing his belongings, and went on his way.

A few minutes later, Moshe saw the gentleman in the dark hat walking slowly up the block.

Here goes, thought Moshe.

"Excuse me, sir," Moshe said to the man, "could you please help me cross the street?"

"Certainly," said the gentleman politely.

"So far, so good," Daniel reported to Uri. "Moshe went over to the man. Now he's speaking to him. I'm getting butterflies in my stomach!

"The man has his hand on Moshe's shoulder. The two are waiting on the curb for the stream of cars to stop so they can cross.

"Now Benny is bending over, reaching in back of the bench."

It took only a few seconds, but to Daniel it seemed like forever. His heart was beating fast. "Benny, why is it taking you so long?" he muttered.

"Finally!" cried Daniel. "Benny is closing his book... he's standing up... he's walking toward the hospital."

A few minutes later, Benny and Moshe came into room 210. Everyone turned to Benny, whose face was white as a sheet.

"Did you find it?" they asked.

"I think so."

Daniel hurried back to the window.

The gentleman in the dark hat sat down on the bench. From time to time, he turned around and looked behind the bench.

"You see," Daniel told his friends. "He seems to be searching for something that was left there for him. I wonder what he'll do when he discovers that it isn't there."

Finally the gentleman in the dark hat stood up, went down the block, got into the white car, and drove off.

Moshe took a memo pad out of his pocket and began to write.

"What are you writing?" asked Uri.

Moshe stood up and showed his friends the memo pad. They read:

765-438-03

"What's that?" asked Benny.

"The license plate number of the white car," said Moshe. Then he wrote next to it: "White Mitsubishi."

"Smart move," Daniel complimented him. "Good job, well done."

"Now tell us," the friends pressed Benny, "what happened?"

"I sat down on the bench," Benny recounted, "and pretended to read a book. Believe me, I was sure the whole street could hear my heart pounding.

"And then," he continued, "out of the corner of my eye, I saw the blind beggar stand up. He came near me, and for a minute I thought he was checking to see whether I noticed what he was doing. Even though he was wearing dark glasses, I felt as if he was looking at me.

"Finally, when he was sure that I wasn't paying attention to him, he bent over the back of the bench."

"And then?" asked Moshe.

"When the beggar turned his back," Benny continued, "I moved slowly toward the edge of the bench and looked down.

"Behind the bench there were empty soda cans and candy wrappers. For a minute, I thought we were mistaken about the whole thing.

"Suddenly I noticed a narrow crack in the wall. Something white was in the crack. It looked like a piece of paper.

"I grabbed it and quickly hid it in the pages of the book. Then I hurried away."

"Show us the paper," said Daniel.

Benny leafed through his book and took something out.

It was a white envelope.

THE MYSTERIOUS ENVELOPE

*M*oshe, Benny, and Daniel gathered around the small cabinet beside Uri's bed. All four boys were staring open-mouthed at the white envelope that Benny had just placed on top of it.

Daniel was the first to recover his power of speech. "Well," he said, "what do you say? Shall we open the envelope?"

"Of course," said Benny. "Isn't that why we took it? It might give us important information about these strange goings-on."

"Moshe," said Daniel, "you have delicate hands. You open the envelope."

Just then Nurse Anat wheeled the medicine wagon into room 210.

"How are you, Daniel?" she called out cheerily, while shaking a bottle of medicine.

"Fine," Daniel replied.

"Oh, I see your friends have come to visit. They've even brought you a letter. Is it from your classmates?"

"N... no," stuttered Daniel in a panic. "I mean, yes. I... I...."

Benny stuck out a nimble hand and gave the medicine wagon a small shove. The precious cargo of medicine bottles and test tubes began to rattle and shake.

"Watch out!" cried Nurse Anat. "You almost knocked everything over!"

She hurried to steady the wagon.

"Okay, no harm done." She sighed in relief. "Come, Daniel, take your medicine so I can move on to the next room."

Nurse Anat handed him a big cup of water and a little cup filled with pink liquid.

Daniel said a prayer over medicine, downed the pink liquid, and sipped a bit of water.

"I tell you," said Nurse Anat to no one in particular, "that child is a *tzaddik*! Whenever I give him medicine, he prays for a speedy recovery."

Pushing the medicine wagon, she left the room. For a while the boys could still hear her mumble to herself, "A *tzaddik*, a real *tzaddik*."

"And now," said Daniel, "the envelope."

This time they closed the privacy curtain that hung around Uri's bed.

Slowly and carefully, Moshe began to open the envelope. He worked so gently that the envelope did not tear.

At last he pulled out a sheet of paper folded in half. He solemnly presented it to Daniel.

Daniel spread the paper open on top of the small cabinet beside Uri's bed.

The paper was blank.

"What is this supposed to be?" asked Benny.

"Just a minute," said Daniel. "Let me examine it."

Daniel looked at the paper from every direction, trying to find the slightest hint of writing.

The paper was entirely blank.

"I must confess," admitted Daniel at last, "that I have no idea what's going on here."

"It *looks* as if certain information is being transmitted," said Uri. "But when the paper falls into our hands, it's blank. So our theory must be mistaken!"

"Not at all," said Daniel thoughtfully. "There's something very mysterious here."

He turned to Uri. "Let me ask you something. Why, in your opinion, would someone put a blank piece of paper in a closed envelope?"

"It really doesn't sound logical," Uri admitted.

"If so," Daniel continued to think aloud, "it must be a signal of some kind."

"Maybe the color of the paper itself is the signal," suggested Moshe.

"Please explain," said Daniel.

"For instance," said Moshe, "if everything is okay, a white paper will be in the envelope, and if there are complications, the paper will be black."

"Very clever," said Benny.

"Moshe just might be right," said Daniel. "We will have to think of more ideas."

The friends sat deep in thought.

Only the ticking of the clock on the wall broke the silence.

SCENTED PAPER

*S*uddenly Daniel jumped up. "I have an idea!"

"We're all ears," said the others.

"There's someone I'd like to let in on our secret," said Daniel, "that is, if you all agree."

"Who?" they wanted to know.

"It's someone I'm sure you've all met," said Daniel. "I was thinking of Mr. Berger."

"Of course we've met him," said Benny. "Who doesn't know good old Mr. Berger."

"You mean the little old man with all the inventions?" asked Moshe.

"That's the one," Daniel confirmed.

"Why do you think we should let him in on the secret?" asked Uri.

"During the time that I've been in the hospital," said Daniel, "I've gotten to know him well. He's very clever and full of original ideas—just the person to help us solve this mystery."

"So you say," Mr. Berger whispered to the group in room 210, "that this happens every single day?"

"Yes," answered Daniel. "The scene has repeated itself for a few days straight."

"So you therefore decided to take action," said Mr. Berger thoughtfully. "But what you discovered was an envelope with a blank sheet of paper. Is that correct?"

"Exactly," the boys confirmed.

"And where is this envelope?" asked Mr. Berger.

"Right here," said Daniel. He pulled it out from under his pillow and handed it to Mr. Berger.

"Just a minute, my boy," said Mr. Berger. "At my age, I must first put on my reading glasses."

The old man took his reading glasses out of his pocket. They traded places with the distance glasses perched precariously on the edge of his nose.

Then he took the envelope and examined it carefully. He held it closer, then farther away. He turned it to every side and looked at it from every angle.

The boys were careful not to disturb him. They did not make a sound.

Finally he took the paper out of the envelope, unfolded it, and repeated the same procedure.

Then, as the boys watched in fascination, he held the paper up to the light, rubbed it gently between his fingers, and finally sniffed it.

"Aha!" A smile spread across his face. "Zalman may be old, but he still knows something."

Benny could restrain himself no longer. "What is it? What did you find?"

Mr. Berger handed the paper to Benny.

"Do you smell anything special?" he asked.

Benny brought the paper up to his nose. It seemed to have a familiar scent. "Maybe it's the smell of a fruit," he said at last, handing the paper to Moshe.

"You're close," said Mr. Berger.

Moshe handed the paper to Uri, who sniffed it carefully. "Lemons!" said Uri. "We have a lemon tree in our yard in Revivim."

"Excellent," said Mr. Berger. "It is indeed the scent of lemons."

"How does that help us?" asked Daniel.

"To answer that question," said Mr. Berger, "I'll need an iron."

"An iron?" asked Moshe in surprise. "Do we need to put on ironed shirts before you explain this mystery to us?"

"Not at all," laughed Mr. Berger. "But it's my fault. I should really explain first things first."

The children listened eagerly. They were careful not to miss one word.

"In the not-so-distant past," Mr. Berger began, "lemon juice was used as invisible ink."

"Invisible ink?" echoed the boys.

"Yes, indeed," replied Mr. Berger. "When you dip a quill into lemon juice, the writing can't be seen on paper."

"If you can't read it, what is it worth?" asked Benny.

"I didn't say you can't read it," said Mr. Berger. "I said only that the writing can't be seen. If you heat the paper slightly, clear, delicate brown writing shows up."

"So that's why we need an iron," said Daniel. "If we heat the paper slightly with the iron, we'll see what's written on it."

"Exactly," confirmed Mr. Berger.

Mrs. Klein had trouble understanding why her son Benny needed an iron in the afternoon instead of a ball, but she was not given to asking many questions.

SECRET CODES

*T*he door of room 210 was closed. Inside, Daniel, Moshe, and Benny were huddled around the small cabinet beside Uri's bed. The mysterious sheet of paper was sitting there on a thick acrylic blanket. In his right hand Mr. Berger held an iron, which he tapped gingerly with the fingertips of his left hand.

"The iron mustn't be too hot," he explained to his young listeners. "Otherwise the letter might burn."

At last Mr. Berger decided that the iron was at just the right temperature. He began to pass it gently over the paper.

Before their eyes, light brown writing began to appear.

"This isn't just a piece of paper," said Uri. "It's a letter!"

When he was finished, Mr. Berger let out a deep sigh. "I hadn't expected *that*," he said.

"What do you mean?" asked Daniel.

"See for yourself," said Mr. Berger, handing him the letter.

Daniel looked at it and then passed it to his friends. There were no words in the letter— only rows of letters and numbers that didn't make any sense.

The boys looked up at Mr. Berger, waiting for him to explain.

"Whoever wrote this message," said Mr. Berger, "wanted to make sure no outsider would understand it. So he used a secret code."

There was a brief silence.

"This is no game," said Mr. Berger at last. "It's clear that someone is trying to pass secret information. There might even be danger involved."

He paused. "It seems to me," Mr. Berger concluded, "that we should go to the police."

"Why not try to crack the code ourselves?" asked Moshe, disappointed.

"Cracking secret codes, my dear young man," explained Mr. Berger, "is no simple matter, especially since there are so many different types. There's only one way to get the job done —and that is to give it to a professional. Besides," he added, "it's not our responsibility."

"I think Mr. Berger is right," said Daniel.

"Okay," said Benny, "let's go to the police."

Police Captain Shimon Suissa sat behind the desk at the police station and eyed the two eleven-year-old boys standing nervously before him. "You say you want to speak to the chief?" he asked.

"Yes," answered Moshe. "we have important information for him."

"First tell me what it's all about," said Suissa. "If I think it's important, I'll pass it on to him."

The two began to tell their story, trying not to leave out any significant details.

"Where is the envelope with this strange letter?" asked Suissa, rubbing his chin skeptically.

"Here it is," said Benny, handing him the envelope.

Suissa took out the letter, unfolded it, and glanced at it briefly.

"Listen carefully, boys," he said sternly. "There seems to be some mischief afoot. I'm not accusing you of fooling around with the police. But someone who likes practical jokes might be playing games with a friend by sending him letters in code.

"Do you really think the police have time to deal with such things?"

With that, Suissa handed the letter back to the boys and dismissed them with a wave of his hand.

❧⟐❧

"I tell you that policeman was wrong," argued Daniel vehemently. "Something illegal is going on right under our noses!"

"That is as clear as day," agreed Benny.

"What do we do next?" asked Moshe. "You heard what Mr. Berger said. It's almost impossible to crack a real code."

"We'll speak to Mr. Berger," said Daniel. "He's sure to give us good advice."

❧⟐❧

Mr. Berger clucked his tongue. "You say the policeman made light of the whole matter?"

"Yes," said Moshe. "He gave us back the letter and sent us away."

"In that case," said Mr. Berger, "there's only one thing to do. We must decipher the secret message. And to do that, we'll have to crack the code ourselves."

"But Mr. Berger," said Daniel, "you told us that's impossible!"

Velvel Weinstein

"The question is for whom," said Mr. Berger. "For you and for me it's impossible. That's why we need the help of Velvel Weinstein."

"Who's he?" asked Daniel.

"An old friend of mine," said Mr. Berger. "During World War II, Velvel was in the British Army. He specialized in deciphering coded broadcasts of the German Army, curses on their heads! For Velvel, cracking codes is child's play."

"Where can we find Mr. Weinstein?" asked Daniel.

"Velvel has a little watch store in Nachalat Shivah, one of Jerusalem's oldest neighborhoods," said Mr. Berger. "Moshe and Benny will have to go to him—if they're willing, of course."

THE WATCHMAKER

$\mathcal{M}$oshe and Benny walked quickly through the old alleys of Nachalat Shivah. Now and then, Moshe patted his pocket to make sure the envelope was safe. They were searching for some trace of Velvel Weinstein's watch store.

Up ahead they spotted an old lady carrying an overflowing shopping basket. She put down the basket and rested for a minute.

The boys hurried over to her. "*Geveret*," they asked politely, "do you know the neighborhood?"

"Do I know the neighborhood?" she said, almost insulted. "You ask Masudah Tuito if she knows the neighborhood? When I was your age I already knew each stone!"

"Do you see that house over there?" Mrs. Tuito continued, pointing to a low stone house. "I was born there, and I've been living there for seventy-three years!"

"May we help you carry your basket home?" Moshe offered.

"You're a dear," said Mrs. Tuito. "Thank you so much!"

Moshe and Benny carried the heavy basket together and walked Mrs. Tuito home.

"We're looking for the watch store," said Benny.

"Of course. Velvel Weinstein's watch store is over there, in the next alley," said Mrs. Tuito, pointing. "I want you to know that Velvel Weinstein is the most honest person I know. You can rely on him. If he tells you a watch is good, you can buy it without any hesitation. Rest assured that it will work well for many years to come."

They reached Mrs. Tuito's front door and deposited the basket there. "Thank you so much," she said. "If only all children were like you!"

***

The watch store was only slightly bigger than a phone booth. Velvel Weinstein himself was sitting behind a small table. He had a watchmaker's magnifying glass in front of his eye, and his attention was fixed on the inner workings of an ancient pocket watch.

Moshe and Benny stood there patiently until the watchmaker noticed them.

"*Shalom*, dear children," he said. "How can I help you?" As he spoke, he removed the magnifying glass from his eye, the better to look at them.

"Uh, we were sent by Mr. Zalman Berger," said Moshe hesitantly. "My name is Moshe, and this is my friend Benny."

"Oh, Zalman, my good old friend!" said the watchmaker happily. "How is he faring?"

"Very well," replied Benny. "He feels fine."

"I should visit him more often," said the watchmaker, "but I'm very busy. And why did he send you to me?"

"We have a secret code for you to crack," said Daniel.

"A secret code?" exclaimed the watchmaker in surprise. "Did one of your classmates send you a message that you can't read? Or are you playing a trick on one another?"

"Neither," said Moshe. "Actually, it's a long story."

And he told the story.

"Where's the letter?" the watchmaker asked when Moshe finished speaking.

"Here it is," said Benny, taking the envelope out of his pocket.

The watchmaker put the magnifying glass near his eye and carefully studied the light brown writing.

The silence was so thick you could almost cut it with a knife.

At last, the watchmaker put the letter down on his table, took off the magnifying glass, and said, "This code was not written by an amateur. It's the work of a professional."

"What's the difference between code written by a professional and code written by an amateur?" asked Benny.

Instead of answering, the watchmaker took out a blank sheet of paper and a pen and gave it to the boys.

"Try to write something in code," he said.

Moshe remembered a code their class had devised. Each letter of the alphabet was replaced by a letter that separated it by an interval of five letters. For *A* they wrote *F*, for *B* they wrote *G*, and for *Z* they wrote *E*.

Moshe worked for a few minutes writing two rows of letters that appeared to be without rhyme or reason. He handed the paper to the watchmaker.

The watchmaker looked at the paper briefly. Then he looked up. "It says: My name is Moshe Goldberg."

The boys were astounded.

"How did you figure it out so quickly?" asked Benny.

"Because it's amateur code," replied the watchmaker. "Amateur code usually contains certain agreed-upon symbols—that is, pictures, numbers, or other letters—to replace the letters of the message.

"And here's another point: Usually, when people are asked to write something, they include their name. I knew that the name Moshe would appear here, since that's how you introduced yourself when you came in.

"Once I found the name Moshe, I figured out what system you used to replace letters. After that, it was easy to read the whole message.

"Professional code," concluded the watchmaker, "is much more complex and sophisticated."

"How much time," asked Benny, "will it take for you to decipher the letter?"

"It's hard to guess," answered the watchmaker. "Anywhere between one hour and a whole month."

A Visit

$\mathcal{T}$he following day, Uri's parents came to visit.

Mr. Segev sat in a wheelchair beside Uri's bed. Mrs. Segev sat on the bed to be as close as possible to her son.

Uri was much improved. His leg had been taken out of traction. According to Dr. Lampert, the young patient would soon be able to walk on crutches.

"I'm so happy," Mrs. Segev told her son lovingly. "I was very worried about you."

No one said so explicitly, but the thought of Uri being confined to a wheelchair like his father was too much to bear.

"Tell us," Mr. Segev asked his son, "what do you do here all day?"

Uri told his father about the new friends he had made in the hospital. He even introduced his parents to Daniel, who had quickly become a close friend. He said nothing about the mystery.

"*Ima*," said Uri. "May I ask you something?"

"Of course, dear," Mrs. Segev replied. "Go right ahead."

"It seems to me," said Uri, "that you and *Abba* are worried. You're hiding something from me, aren't you?"

Mr. and Mrs. Segev exchanged silent glances. "Ilana," he said, "you tell him."

Mrs. Segev drew a deep breath. "We weren't planning to tell you," she said. "But I see you sensed it anyway.

"You know that *Abba* has suffered pain ever since he was wounded. But recently it's gotten much worse, and he may need a complicated operation.

"The problem is," Mrs. Segev continued, "that there is a difference of opinion among the doctors. Some are in favor of the operation. Others are opposed—they say an operation will only make things worse."

Mrs. Segev wiped a tear from the corner of her eye. Uri turned as white as the pillowcase under his head.

"Don't worry, my boy," said Mr. Segev, patting his hand. "Everything will turn out all right."

Nighttime. The hospital slept. Here and there a monitor buzzed and an infusion device dripped. From time to time, a groan was heard from one of the rooms as a patient tried to find a more comfortable position. A small light was on at the nurses' station, where the nurses on duty chatted quietly.

In room 210, a sound woke Daniel up. He opened his eyes and listened.

The sound was coming from the direction of Uri's bed. Uri was crying!

Daniel got out of bed and quietly approached his friend's bed. He brought over a chair and sat down.

"What happened, Uri?" asked Daniel carefully.

Uri wiped his eyes and was silent.

"Tell me, Uri," Daniel pressed gently. "Maybe I can help you!"

I'm lucky to have such a wonderful friend, Uri thought, *but how can he possibly help me?*

Finally, Uri told his story, interrupted occasionally by the tears that choked his throat.

When Uri finished his story, he felt greatly relieved. He himself didn't even know why.

"I know what to do!" said Daniel.

"What *is* there to do?" asked Uri.

"Listen," said Daniel. "Have you ever heard of an organization called Refuah?"

"No," said Uri.

"Let me explain," said Daniel. "Unfortunately, many people who suffer from medical problems don't know what to do or where to turn for help."

"True," agreed Uri.

"That's why," continued Daniel enthusiastically, "the rabbis have started *chesed* organizations that specialize in medical advice. These organizations can contact experts anywhere in the world who specialize in treating a particular problem.

"And it doesn't end there," continued Daniel. "If necessary, these *chesed* organizations fly the patient to a different country where he will receive the best treatment. They even arrange lodging for the patient and the relatives who accompany him."

"Absolutely unbelievable!" exclaimed Uri.

"If you're interested," said Daniel, "I'll put you in touch with Rabbi Gershon Wolf, the head of Refuah."

"Of course I'm interested," said Uri. "I'm sure my dad will be happy to consult him. But how do you contact Rabbi Wolf?"

"I'll call him immediately!"

"Do you know what time it is?" said Uri. "It's after 2 o'clock in the morning!"

"I know," said Daniel, "but to Rabbi Wolf and his helpers, the evening has just begun!"

Daniel went to his bedside cabinet, took out the cellular phone his parents had given him for his hospital stay, leafed through a phone book, and dialed.

"Refuah, *shalom*," said a pleasant voice. "How may we help you?"

"May I speak to Rabbi Wolf, please?"

"About what?" asked the rabbi's secretary.

Daniel outlined the problem in brief and was asked to wait.

"What's happening?" asked Uri.

"They're transferring me to Rabbi Wolf," said Daniel.

"Gershon here," said a voice that was warm and pleasant. "How can I help you?"

Daniel told the story briefly.

"I'll need all the results of the patient's tests and x-rays," said Rabbi Wolf. "Please fax me the material, and I'll get back to you as soon as possible."

"Thank you so much," answered Daniel, deeply moved.

"It's nothing," said Rabbi Wolf, and went on to the next person who needed his help.

ANGELS IN WHITE JACKETS

*G*iora Segev gave in to his son's pleas and sent his test results to Refuah. As soon as the fax came in to Refuah's modest office in Jerusalem, Rabbi Wolf placed a conference call to three orthopedic surgeons: one in Washington, a second in South Africa, and a third in France. They discussed Segev's problem together, after which Rabbi Wolf summarized the main points and thanked them warmly.

Rabbi Wolf picked up the phone again and called Revivim. "I've spoken to a number of world-famous specialists," Rabbi Wolf told Segev. "All of them recommended going ahead with the operation. They see no reason to put it off.

"You can have it done next Wednesday," Rabbi Wolf continued, "by Dr. George Johnson."

"Next Wednesday?" echoed Segev in amazement. "How can we get ready so quickly?"

"Don't worry," said Rabbi Wolf. "Refuah will take care of all the arrangements."

"In what hospital will it be done?" asked Segev.

"Dr. Johnson is the head of orthopedics in Merkin Hospital in Washington D.C.," said Rabbi Wolf. "His success in the operating room has given him the reputation as one of the greatest orthopedists in the world.

"We're believing Jews," Rabbi Wolf added. "We hope that Dr. Johnson will be a good messenger of *Hashem*."

"I'm really very grateful," said Segev. "But I'm afraid that in my present condition, I won't be able to fly."

"Don't worry about anything," said Rabbi Wolf. "Leave all the arrangements to me and my devoted staff. You'll fly in a special section of the plane, in a bed as comfortable as your bed at home. A doctor will accompany you. When you arrive in Washington, Refuah volunteers will be waiting to take you to the hospital.

"By the way," concluded Rabbi Wolf, "a room will be booked for your wife in a hotel near the hospital."

"I don't know how I can ever thank you," said Segev.

Ilana Segev faced a dilemma. On the one hand, she could not let her husband undergo an operation alone in a foreign country. On the other hand, how could she leave her eleven-year-old son alone in an Israeli hospital while she went to the United States?

"*Ima*," said Uri, "you go with *Abba*. I'm not alone here in room 210. Daniel, Moshe, and Benny are with me. They'll help me with everything. Don't worry about me."

The decision was difficult, but there was no choice. Mrs. Segev would join her husband, but Aunt Chagit would keep in touch with Uri and visit him from time to time.

Giora Segev had flown many times, but this was one flight he would never forget.

The Refuah ambulance came to his house to take him to the airport in maximum comfort. The ambulance driver and his assistant, white-jacketed men with beards and *peyos*, transferred him gently and skillfully from the wheelchair to the bed in the ambulance.

It's amazing how these two treat me, thought Segev. What loving concern! It's so important to them that I shouldn't suffer at all. You would think I was a member of their own family—but they don't even know me.

They're angels.

Angels in white jackets.

WHO KNOWS GIDON?

*D*aniel sat in bed one afternoon studying Mishnah, trying to catch up to his class before he returned to school.

Suddenly he heard a cheerful voice warmly wishing the
young patients a speedy recovery. The voice came closer.

"Shalom, dear children," the voice boomed, as Mr. Berger
entered room 210. "I've brought you a guest."

Daniel and Uri looked curiously toward the doorway.

"Come in, come in," Mr. Berger urged the guest.

Into the room walked a man about the same age as Mr.
Berger.

"Let me introduce you to a dear old friend," said Mr.
Berger. "This is Velvel Weinstein, the watchmaker from
Nachalat Shivah."

Daniel almost fell off the bed.

"Shalom," said the watchmaker. "I've had the privilege of
meeting your fine friends Moshe and Benny, and now I'm
pleased to meet you."

"Mr. Weinstein has news for us," said Mr. Berger. "He came
to deliver it personally."

Daniel and Uri waited tensely to hear what the watchmaker would say.

"I managed to decipher the letter," said Mr. Weinstein simply.
"But I think Moshe and Benny should be here when I read it."

Daniel quickly phoned Benny's house. Benny's father drove him and Moshe to the hospital.

❧❧❧

"Cracking the code wasn't easy," the watchmaker began. "Since the code is a combination of letters and numbers, I had to try various methods.

"Many times," he explained, "the two sides—that is, the sender of the message and the receiver—own a certain book. The numbers represent the page of the book, the line, and the word on the line. The receiver can decode the letter with little effort."

"In that case," observed Daniel, "we would only need to know what book they were using. The rest would be easy."

"That's right," agreed the watchmaker. "But in our case, the method was entirely different. Would you like me to explain how it works?"

"Yes!" said the boys eagerly.

"Pay careful attention, then," said the watchmaker, as he took a large sheet of paper and a pen out of his pocket.

"Let's say I want to write the following statement: 'Message confirmed. Enemy to land on coast next Tuesday.' First I would run all the letters together, in lower case, with no spaces or periods, like so:

messageconfirmedenemytolandoncoastnexttuesday

"Next, I would break the sentence up into rows. But first I would have to decide how many letters I wanted in a row.

"Then I would write one row from left to right, the other from right to left.

"For instance, if I decided on a row of nine letters, I would write it this way:

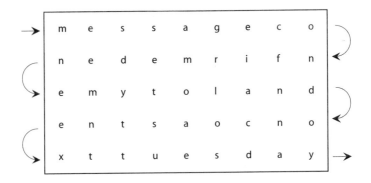

m	e	s	s	a	g	e	c	o
n	e	d	e	m	r	i	f	n
e	m	y	t	o	l	a	n	d
e	n	t	s	a	o	c	n	o
x	t	t	u	e	s	d	a	y

"Now, if I wanted to add another level of difficulty—to make sure no one could read it—I would encode it again, this time diagonally, like so:

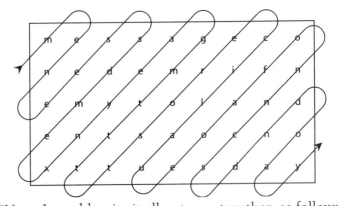

"Next, I would write it all out, run together, as follows: **meneessdmexnyeagmttttsorecilaneoafonncsdudaay**

"Finally, I would put the letters in rows of nine letters, as agreed upon in advance. It would then look like this:

m	e	n	e	e	s	s	d	m
e	x	n	y	e	a	g	m	t
t	t	t	s	o	r	e	c	i
l	a	n	e	o	a	f	o	n
n	c	s	d	n	d	a	a	y

"In order to read the message, I would have to go through all the stages again, but this time in reverse. In this format," concluded the watchmaker, "it is very difficult to crack the code."

"Difficult?" said Uri. "Why, it's impossible! How did you do it?"

"I told you," said Mr. Berger cheerfully, thumping his friend on the shoulder, "Velvel Weinstein is a true expert. I knew he wouldn't let anything stand in his way."

Daniel was the first to recover his composure. "If you've cracked the code, Mr. Weinstein," he said, "please tell us what the letter says!"

"Oh, of course," said the watchmaker. He took a carefully folded paper from his pocket and handed it to Uri. "Read it to them."

Mr. Berger and the boys huddled around Uri, who read:

"Gidon is arriving at eight and leaving at six-thirty. Evidently the date is suitable. Await instructions."

"Who is Gidon?" asked Daniel.

"I have no idea," said the watchmaker. "But one thing is sure: the matter is very serious. However, I have done my part, and with that, my duty ends. If you need any additional help, don't hesitate to turn to me again."

The watchmaker stood up and took his hat. Mr. Berger and the boys thanked him warmly as he waved good-bye and left.

"He's something special, isn't he?" said Mr. Berger with delight. "If you have a letter to be deciphered, Velvel Weinstein is your man!"

"Astounding," said Uri. "But where do we go from here?"

The four boys and the old man sat in silence, deep in thought.

DIFFICULT DECISIONS

"In my opinion," said Mr. Berger, breaking the silence that had settled over room 210, "there is espionage afoot."

The boys looked at him in surprise.

"Apparently this blind beggar—who, by the way, may not be blind at all—is passing information to another party. The information is about a person known as Gidon."

"What do you mean by 'a person known as Gidon'?" asked Daniel.

"Gidon may not be his real name," Mr. Berger replied. "It may be a code name for someone else."

"But how does the information about Gidon get to the blind beggar?" asked Moshe. "Does he gather it himself? Or does he get it from someone else?"

"Good question," said Daniel.

"By the way," put in Uri, "what makes you think it's espionage? Maybe a gang of thieves is planning a robbery, and Gidon is their victim."

"There's only one way to find out," said Mr. Berger pensively, "but I'm not sure I want to tell you what it is."

"Mr. Berger!" the boys clamored together. "Please don't leave us in suspense."

Mr. Berger hesitated a moment. Finally he said, "If we want to solve the mystery, we have to tail the blind beggar."

"Wow!" exclaimed Moshe. "Just like in books."

"In books it's simple," said Mr. Berger. "But in reality, it can be very dangerous. Besides, if the blind beggar and his gang are professional spies, they'll shake us off their tracks before we discover anything."

"What shall we do?" asked Uri.

"Maybe I'll go speak with Velvel Weinstein tomorrow," said Mr. Berger. "His knowledge and experience may be of help to us."

Noontime in Nachalat Shivah. Velvel Weinstein's fingers drummed on the small table.

Across from him, Zalman Berger sat silently on a stool, waiting to hear his reaction.

"Look, Zalman," said the watchmaker. "I'm not going to tell you whether or not to shadow those men. The decision is up to you. But if you're interested, I'm willing to teach you some basic rules about how to do it. Write them down and study them well."

Mr. Berger nodded his consent. He took out a notepad and pen and listened carefully.

"First of all," said the watchmaker, "take along one of the children. You'll look like a grandfather strolling with his grandson.

"Second, try to blend in with the crowd. Don't wear clothing that's conspicuous.

"Third, keep your distance from the suspect. Don't get too close to him.

"Fourth, if the suspect stops suddenly in front of a store window, hide quickly. He's looking at the reflection in the window to check whether he's being followed.

"Fifth...

In room 210, the boys listened open-mouthed as Mr. Berger read them his notes.

When he finished, there was silence in the room.

"What do you say?" asked Mr. Berger.

"We need a volunteer," said Daniel. "Unfortunately, Uri and I can't leave the hospital, so it will have to be either Moshe or Benny."

Moshe and Benny looked at one another.

"Why don't the two of you go together?" asked Uri.

"Excellent," said Benny. "We'll look like grandchildren out strolling with their grandfather."

"Agreed?" asked Mr. Berger.

"Agreed," answered Moshe and Benny bravely.

"We begin tomorrow. We'll follow the blind beggar when he leaves his position down there," said Mr. Berger, nodding toward the window.

In a small private home on the outskirts of Jerusalem, the phone rang.

The caller was sitting in a spacious office in London. "It's me," he said, without any preliminary remarks. "Anything new?"

"Everything is going as planned," replied the man in Jerusalem. "A lot of information is already in our hands. We're missing only a few details before we can put the final touches on the operation."

"What about the missing envelope?" asked the man in London grimly. "Have you found out where it disappeared to?"

"Not yet," admitted the man in Jerusalem. "It may have blown away in the wind. We're looking into it."

The caller hung up without saying good-bye.

PRAYER

*T*he guard politely asked all visitors to leave the children's ward. It was time for the young patients to go to sleep. A friend who had been helping Daniel study Mishnah said good-bye and went home.

Uri lay in bed thinking.

"You know," said Uri, "it's tomorrow."

"What's tomorrow?" asked Daniel, his mind still on the Mishnah open before him.

"Tomorrow is my father's operation," said Uri.

"What?" Daniel jumped up. "The operation is tomorrow? Why didn't you tell me?"

"I'm telling you now," said Uri.

Daniel drew a chair close to Uri's bed.

"It feels strange," Uri continued. "Tomorrow is a fateful day for my family."

"What are you planning to do tomorrow?" asked Daniel.

"What is there to do?" asked Uri.

Daniel said gently, "Your father will need a lot of help from *Hashem*. Tomorrow we must pray together for his recovery."

The idea was entirely new to Uri. Nevertheless, he felt he wanted to pray.

"Let's start by saying a chapter of *Tehillim* for him right now," Daniel suggested.

Uri agreed willingly.

Daniel handed Uri a yarmulka, and Uri put it on his head.

Daniel leafed through the little Book of *Tehillim* that he always kept with him, and the two young boys read together, "*Shir hama'alos, mima'amakim....*"

Uri felt like a son pleading with his Father in Heaven. At last, he had Someone to turn to!

When they finished, he asked Daniel to read another chapter of *Tehillim* with him.

7:00 in the morning.

In the Goldberg home, the telephone rang. "Moshe!" called Mrs. Goldberg. "You have a phone call!"

"Moshe," said Daniel, "the operation is today. Please arrange for *Tehillim* to be said in school for Uri's father. His name is Giora ben Sarah."

"Good morning, Mom," said Daniel. "How are you?"

"Are you all right, Daniel?" Mrs. Green asked worriedly. "What are you calling about so early in the morning? Did anything happen last night?"

"No, nothing at all," said Daniel to calm her. "I just wanted to ask you to pray for Uri's father. The operation is today. Maybe Dad's yeshivah can say *Tehillim*."

"Sure," said Mrs. Green, as she jotted down "Giora ben Sarah."

In Washington D.C.'s Merkin Hospital, Ilana Segev sat with clasped hands in the waiting room outside the operating suite. Her husband had just been wheeled inside.

Dr. George Johnson, head of the orthopedic department, arrived in his green surgical uniform. Mrs. Segev hurried toward him.

"Doctor," she said worriedly, "please do whatever you can to help my husband!"

Dr. Johnson's only answer was to point a figure upward. Experience had proven to him that the world had a Creator Who guided the surgical knife in his hands. "Pray!" he said.

Then he disappeared behind the operating room's swinging doors, which continued to swing for a few moments afterward.

Mrs. Segev went over to the public phone, put in a handful of coins, and dialed.

"Uri," she said emotionally, "they're starting the operation." She wanted to say more, but tears choked her throat.

"*Ima*," said Uri, "pray to *Hashem*! I'm finding out that everything depends on Him!"

A MIRACLE

*T*ime passed slowly. The hands of the clock stopped moving—or so it seemed to Ilana Segev. "The operation may take several hours," a nurse had told her.

The waiting room was filled with people of different colors and languages. They had one thing in common: All were waiting tensely for a surgeon to come through the swinging doors and tell them how their loved one was faring.

"Mrs. Segev," said the Refuah volunteer who had offered to wait with Ilana during those difficult hours, "would you like something to eat?"

"No, thank you," said Mrs. Segev. "I have no appetite."

Then she recalled Uri's request. "But perhaps you could help me say a chapter of *Tehillim*?"

The students of Jerusalem's Noam Torah Yeshivah had just finished *Minchah*. The Rosh Yeshivah Rabbi Reuven Green, Daniel's father, handed the *chazzan* a piece of paper that said, "Giora ben Sarah."

The *chazzan* banged on the table. The students understood the signal. They were about to say *Tehillim* for the recovery of a sick person.

"*Maskil l'David* ..." the *chazzan* began.

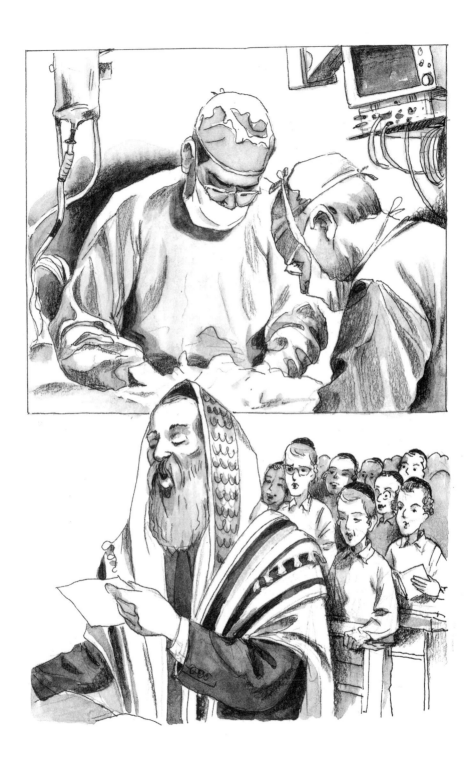

The students repeated the verses after him with a mighty cry—the type of cry that bursts from the heart, breaks through the heavens, and rips up painful decrees.

"Mrs. Segev!" called the nurse.

"Yes!" Mrs. Segev responded. "That's me!" She braced herself for the news.

"Don't worry," the nurse said soothingly. "I just wanted to tell you that the operation is over."

"How is he? Was the operation successful? Did it go well?"

"I'm not authorized to say anything," said the nurse. "But soon Dr. Johnson will come out and speak to you about your husband's condition."

"Mrs. Segev!" called the nurse, later. "Dr. Johnson would like you to come to his office."

Ilana Segev hurried down the long corridor, which seemed endless. At last she found herself seated in the spacious office, facing the surgeon who had just finished operating on her husband.

Dr. Johnson was on the phone. She tried to read his expression. Was there a smile of satisfaction on his face, or was it wishful thinking?

After a few minutes that seemed like an eternity, he hung up.

"Mrs. Segev," Dr. Johnson began, "I am pleased to inform you that the operation was more successful than we dared hope."

Ilana Segev could not believe her ears. Was this really happening, or was it a dream? Tears of joy filled her eyes. "What do you mean?" she finally managed to ask.

"There is a reasonable chance," said Dr. Johnson, "that your husband may eventually be able to walk again.

"Of course," the surgeon continued, "he will have to undergo a long period of rehabilitation and physiotherapy. But I believe that after it is completed, he will walk normally."

The phone at Uri's bedside rang.

His mother sounded happier than she'd been in a long time. "Uri," she said, "we've had a miracle! The operation was successful! *Abba* may even be able to walk again one day!"

The good news spread like wildfire. Mr. Berger ran to buy a bottle of soda and a box of chocolates, Nurse Anat brought cookies, and Moshe and Benny hurried over with balloons. For a long time, children and nurses on the ward kept coming in to wish Uri mazal tov.

When the visitors finally left and the echoes of joy had subsided, Uri and Daniel chatted quietly together.

"Even though I've only known you for a short time," said Uri, "I feel as if you're my best friend. I'm forever grateful for your help."

"Don't talk nonsense," said Daniel hoarsely. "I didn't do anything special."

"You were so supportive when I was down," said Uri. "And so were Moshe and Benny. I even told my mother, when she was afraid to leave me, that I'm not alone. I have good friends here with me."

For a few minutes, the two were silent.

After a while, Daniel saw that his friend had dropped off to sleep. *He must be worn out from all the tension and excitement,* thought Daniel.

He got up quietly and shut the light over Uri's bed.

Tailing the Blind Beggar

The schoolyard was exploding with the energy of children letting off steam at recess. Some had organized a ball game; others were playing tag.

Two were whispering in a corner.

"Tell me the truth," said Moshe. "Aren't you afraid?"

"What's there to be afraid of?" asked Benny. "All in all, we're going to tail a blind beggar. What's so dangerous about that?"

"Even so," replied Moshe.

"If you're worried," suggested Benny, "I'll go with Mr. Berger myself."

"Oh, no," said Moshe quickly. "You can't leave me out of this exciting adventure!"

The bell rang, cutting the conversation short. Benny and Moshe hurried back to class.

At 5 o'clock the group assembled in room 210. Mr. Berger laid out a detailed operational plan and gave final instructions.

Moshe handed Daniel a small pair of binoculars that he had brought from home. Now Daniel could watch from the window.

Ten to 6.

"Boys," said Mr. Berger as he put on his hat, "prepare to move."

At 6 o'clock sharp, the beggar went over to the green bench, as expected.

"There's the man in the dark hat," said Moshe. "He's walking up the block."

The man sauntered over to the bench, sat down, and looked around. Then he reached casually behind the bench. Finally, he stood up and left.

"Come, boys," said Mr. Berger. "We're going out for a walk."

The three left the hospital exactly as the blind beggar got up, gathered his cane and plastic bag, straightened his dark glasses, and began to slowly make his way down the block, tapping with his cane as he went.

They waited until he was a safe distance away. Then the three, hearts pounding, walked after him.

A few minutes later, the blind beggar suddenly turned into the doorway of a small apartment building.

"Does he live there?" asked Moshe.

"I don't know," said Mr. Berger. "Benny, walk on ahead, pass by the entrance, and see whether he's going up the stairs."

Benny quickened his pace. As he passed the entrance, he saw the blind beggar standing in the stairwell. His back was to the entrance.

Benny pretended to be studying a notice posted on a tree. Out of the corner of his eye, he saw the blind beggar take off his tattered coat, fold it carefully, and put it into the bag. From the bag he took out a nice sweater, which he put on. He folded his cane and removed the dark glasses. These articles, too, went into the bag. Then the beggar went back out to the street.

Mr. Berger and Moshe did not recognize the sighted man in the nice sweater who emerged from the apartment building entrance. Benny's nervous signals told them that it was the "blind" beggar.

The man in the nice sweater walked slowly down the street, peering occasionally into store windows.

"He isn't interested in what the store is selling," Mr. Berger told the boys quietly. "He's checking to see whether he's being followed. We'll have to be doubly careful."

Suddenly the beggar extended his hand, and a grey taxi pulled up beside him. The beggar got in, and the taxi took off.

"Hello, taxi!" hollered Mr. Berger, as he waved his hand desperately.

A taxi stopped for them. "Get in quickly, boys," Mr. Berger ordered.

"Where to?" asked the driver.

"Do you see that grey taxi up ahead?" he asked.

"Yes, of course," said the driver, surprised.

"Excellent," said Mr. Berger. "Follow it, but make sure they don't find out. A friend of ours is in that cab, and we want to surprise him in honor of his birthday."

"Ah," said the driver, pleased to cooperate, "ask any taxi driver in Jerusalem, and you'll hear who Avshalom is! I have a lot of experience tailing people. You're just playing games, but I've helped the police shadow suspects!"

"Very nice," said Mr. Berger. "Just don't lose sight of the grey taxi."

"Depend on me," said the driver. "No one escapes from Avshalom!"

The grey taxi left the center of town and headed toward the outskirts. There it went up a hill and stopped in front of a small private home on Kinor Street.

"What now? asked Avshalom. "Do you want to get out and surprise him?"

"No!" said Mr. Berger. "He mustn't see us now, or else the whole surprise will be ruined. Please let us off around the corner."

As Avshalom continued, the group turned their heads. They watched as the beggar got out of the grey taxi and opened the gate to the yard.

A grandfather and his two grandsons got out of a taxi and strolled toward Kinor Street. The grandfather seemed to be pointing out the plants and flowers to his grandsons. He also showed them a small playground with brightly colored swings and slides on the other side of the street.

"The next house is the blind beggar's," whispered Mr. Berger. "Watch for identifying signs."

Number 37 Kinor Street was a small private house surrounded by a neglected yard. In front of the house stood a rusty brown mailbox bearing the inscription "Jerry Thompson."

ON BICYCLES

*I*n front of one of the houses on Kinor Street, a man was trimming a hedge. His pruning shears made quick, skillful slashes in the bushes.

"Come, boys," whispered Mr. Berger. "This is a wonderful opportunity to gather information."

"Good afternoon, sir," Mr. Berger called out. "We heard there is a house for sale on this block. Do you know anything about it?"

"Could be," the man answered politely. "From time to time I hear that one of my neighbors wants to sell his house, but at the moment I can't think of anyone who does."

"What kind of street is this?" asked Mr. Berger. "Are the neighbors here nice?"

"Very nice, quiet people," answered the man. "Each one keeps to himself. A doctor and his wife live in the house opposite"—he pointed—"and I haven't the slightest idea whether they're here in Israel or abroad on vacation."

"Do you know everyone on the block?" asked Mr. Berger carefully.

"Almost all," he replied.

Mr. Berger pretended to look for a note in his pocket. "The real estate agent told me," said Mr. Berger, "that 35 or 37 Kinor Street is for sale. Do you know who lives at those addresses?"

"Number 35 belongs to Mr. Silver," the man replied. "I'm sure he's not interested in selling. Only yesterday he asked if I could recommend an interior decorator. He wants to renovate his house."

"And what about 37?" asked Mr. Berger.

"The owner of 37 is an eccentric bachelor. I don't even know his name—something like Lawson. He's a quiet person who hardly ever shows his face in the neighborhood, except for 7:30 every morning, when he goes out for a ride on his bike. I wouldn't be at all surprised if he decided to sell his house."

"Thank you so much," said Mr. Berger in parting. "You've been very helpful."

"It was nothing," smiled the man. "Your grandsons are wonderfully patient. They don't tug at your sleeves like mine do if I stop for a minute to chat."

"Yes," said Mr. Berger proudly. "They really are good boys."

An hour later, Mr. Berger, Moshe, and Benny were back in room 210. Uri and Daniel listened wide-eyed to the details of the adventure. They heaped praises on Benny for shadowing the blind beggar in the stairwell.

"If not for you," Mr. Berger told Benny, "we would have lost our beggar. Now we even know his name and address!"

"You did a great job yourself, Mr. Berger," said Uri. "The story about the real estate agent was very creative."

"What next?" asked Daniel, practical as always.

"Next," answered Mr. Berger, "we have to tail the phony beggar. We know that every morning at 7:30 he goes for a ride on his bike. We must find out where he goes.

"But that is something only I can do," continued Mr. Berger, "since Moshe and Benny have school. I don't want them to miss learning Torah."

"Tomorrow we have a class trip," said Moshe. "Nothing will happen if we miss it."

"Very well," said Mr. Berger. "If so, I have a plan for you."

"What is it?" asked Moshe.

"Tomorrow morning," said Mr. Berger, "you and Benny will go bike riding."

Besides the brightly colored swings and slides, there were also two bicycles in the playground on Kinor Street early that morning. Two boys wearing safety helmets were bent over, carefully examining the front wheel of one of the bicycles.

Actually, Benny's attention was riveted to the house across the street.

"Do you have the cell phone so we can call Mr. Berger?" asked Moshe.

"Yes," said Benny.

The rusty iron gate of the house at 37 Kinor Street squeaked open. Jerry Thompson emerged, pushing a bicycle ahead of him. A straw hat lent him the appearance of a nature-lover going out for a refreshing morning ride.

"Here he comes," whispered Benny excitedly. "Get ready."

Thompson got on his bike and took off.

The boys waited until he was a safe distance away. Then they got on their bikes and took off in pursuit.

The cellular phone in Benny's pocket rang.

"What's doing?" asked Mr. Berger, sounding worried. "Did the rider set out yet?"

"Yes," replied Benny, "and we're on his trail."

"Be very careful," he warned. "Call me as soon as you think he's reached his destination."

"You can rely on us," said Benny.

"I know," said Mr. Berger. "Nevertheless, take good care of yourselves, and don't perform any heroic feats."

Jerry Thompson rode his bicycle into town.

After a 20-minute ride, he stopped on a busy street full of bus stops, stores, buildings, and crowds of people.

Thompson got off his bicycle and walked it for a while until he reached a shady bench. Then he leaned his bicycle against a tree and sat down.

Moshe and Benny, too, got off their bicycles, which they parked and locked in a narrow alley. Out of the corners of their eyes they studied Thompson, twenty-five yards away.

Benny dialed.

Mr. Berger answered immediately. "Hello. Where are you?"

"In front of 176 Melech Street," said Benny.

"I'll be there in 5 minutes," said Mr. Berger.

"Why do you think he's sitting there?" asked Moshe.

"Maybe he's waiting for someone," answered Benny thoughtfully. "Or else—or else he's watching something."

"Such as?" prompted Moshe.

"Let's put ourselves into his shoes for a minute," said Benny. "Let's assume that he chose that bench deliberately, not by accident. Why? What does a person see when he sits on that bench?"

"He sees the bus stop next to him," said Moshe, "and the buildings across the street."

"So," said Benny, "he may be waiting for someone to get off a bus or come out of a building."

A taxi pulled up and Mr. Berger hurried out.

"I was a little worried about you," said Mr. Berger, panting. "What's doing?"

The two showed him where Jerry Thompson was sitting and shared their thoughts.

"Very good," said Mr. Berger. "But I want to think for a minute."

The boys looked at their friend. They could almost hear his sharp mind in action.

At last Mr. Berger put his hand into his jacket. From one of his many pockets he took out a pair of tiny folding binoculars. He put them to his eyes and looked cautiously across at the other side of the street.

"Aha!" he said finally. "That's it."

"What's it?" the boys asked.

"See for yourselves," said Mr. Berger, handing them the binoculars.

"Do you see the buildings there, exactly opposite the bench on which Thompson is sitting?" he asked.

A group of tall buildings were surrounded by a high fence. In the fence was a wide opening, blocked by an electric gate. Beside the gate was a small guardhouse.

"Do you mean the buildings with the electric gate and the guard?" the boys asked.

"Precisely," said Mr. Berger. "Look, at the right side of the gate there's a small sign. Read what it says."

The boys looked through the binoculars.

A small, shiny copper sign read, "State of Israel— Department of Defense."

THE LIMOUSINE

A meeting was convened in room 210.

Daniel and Uri listened in amazement as Moshe and Benny reported on their morning bicycle ride. Mr. Berger added his own comments.

"It seems," said Daniel, "that Jerry Thompson has set his sights on the Department of Defense. What do you think he's looking for there?"

"Good question," said Mr. Berger. "He can't get into the complex itself, since a soldier is stationed at the entrance. The soldier certainly won't let anyone in without proper identification."

"Maybe Thompson has proper identification," suggested Moshe.

"I'm sure he does," said Mr. Berger. "But at the entrance to a defense installation, they don't request only papers; they also want to know the purpose of your visit."

"That's how it is in Revivim, too," added Uri. "No one can get in unless he identifies himself and states the purpose of his visit."

"What happens if guests come to visit your family?" asked Moshe.

"The guard at the entrance of the base asks them what their purpose is in coming," said Uri. "When they answer that they're visiting the Segev family, the guard calls us to confirm that we really are expecting guests by that name."

Benny brought the subject back to the matter at hand. "So what is Jerry Thompson looking for when he sits across from the Defense Department complex?"

"Try to recall," Mr. Berger encouraged them. "Did you notice anything strange or unusual while he was sitting on the bench? Did he do anything?"

Benny and Moshe silently replayed the scene in their minds.

"Nothing," they concluded at last.

"Tomorrow morning," said Mr. Berger, "I'll wait for Thompson next to the Defense Department complex."

Night.

At 37 Kinor Street, the phone rang.

The master of the house rose from his armchair and picked up the receiver.

"How are things going?" asked the man from London.

Thompson replied with a few words.

"Are you being followed?" asked the man from London.

"Perhaps," said Thompson hesitantly. "I'm not sure."

"Be ten times as careful now as you were before," the man from London ordered. "We're very close to our goal. Make sure nothing and nobody stops us from accomplishing it."

"Okay," said Thompson. "I'll take care of it."

"Would you like me to get you help from The Friend?" asked the man from London.

"Not now," said Thompson. "Not yet."

A click indicated that the man from London had hung up. As usual, he had not said good-bye.

Jerry Thompson returned to his armchair.

Early in the morning, Melech Street throbbed with people. Some waited for buses, others hurried into the office buildings that lined the street, while yet others stopped at a coffee shop for a cup of steaming coffee and fragrant fresh cake. The waiter in the coffee shop waved cheerily to a sanitation worker sweeping the sidewalk.

Two old men, absorbed in a game of chess, sat on opposite sides of a small stone table. From this position, Velvel Weinstein and Zalman Berger had a good view of the bench.

At 10 to 8, Thompson got off his bicycle and walked it a bit. Finally he stopped beside "his" bench, leaned his bicycle against the tree, and sat down.

Long moments passed, and nothing happened.

"What is he thinking about for so long?" Mr. Berger hissed between his teeth.

"Don't despair," the watchmaker told him. "Following a suspect can take a very long time. Be patient."

At 8:01, it happened.

A black limousine inched its way slowly through the heavy traffic. Thompson tensed.

"There it goes," observed Mr. Berger.

Thompson reached into his briefcase and took out a silver cigarette lighter. Then he put a cigarette into his mouth and lit it.

The black limousine slowed down and turned toward the Defense Department complex.

Thompson again lit the cigarette with his lighter.

The black limousine pulled up before the electric gate.

Thompson stood up. Once again, he lit the cigarette.

The soldier recognized the passenger. He quickly opened the gate, and the black limousine rolled into the complex.

"Did you see what Thompson was doing?" asked the watchmaker.

"Not really," admitted Mr. Berger. "I noticed only one thing: when the black limousine arrived, our man looked very tense."

"Correct," said the watchmaker, "but there's much more."

"Why," said Mr. Berger. "What did you see?"

"When the car arrived," said the watchmaker, "Thompson took a cigarette lighter out of his briefcase. Then he examined the car from every angle."

Mr. Berger looking curiously at his friend.

"Did you notice," the watchmaker continued to ask, "how many times he lit the cigarette that was in his mouth?"

"Why is that significant?" asked Mr. Berger. "So what if the cigarette didn't light well?"

"The cigarette lit perfectly well," said the watchmaker. "But in my opinion, the lighter is not what it appears to be."

"What do you mean?" asked Mr. Berger.

"I suspect," said the watchmaker, "that inside the lighter there's a hidden camera. That's why Thompson lit the cigarette when he saw the black limousine approaching—he was photographing the limousine. He did the same thing twice more."

"If so," said Mr. Berger, "we're dealing with a spy who uses a hidden camera!"

"Of course," said the watchmaker. "Did you think he would stand in the middle of town with a big camera, for everyone to see what he's up to?"

Thompson stood up. He was pleased; he had accomplished his mission. Suddenly his eyes caught sight of two old men, deep in conversation, who were sitting not far from him. One of them looked away quickly when their eyes met.

Where have I seen that old man? Thompson mused. I'm sure I've met him before....

Before getting back on his bicycle, Thompson pretended to rummage through his briefcase. Meanwhile, he took the lighter and photographed the old man a few times.

If he's the one who's tailing me, thought Thompson, The Friend will take care of him.

REUNIONS AND PARTINGS

*A*unt Chagit decorated room 210 with flowers and balloons. Uri's mother was flying in from America. From the airport she would come straight to Bikurim Hospital.

There was another cause for excitement as well. For the first time since the accident, Dr. Lampert allowed Uri to get out of bed.

Mrs. Segev, wheeling a large suitcase, walked into room 210—and found Uri sitting in an armchair. Tears of joy rolled down her cheeks as she hugged her beloved son.

Excitement filled the room and overflowed into the corridor. The good news spread quickly through the children's ward.

From the corridor, Moshe and Benny already noticed that something was afoot. The door to room 210 was covered with colorful balloons and a big "Welcome" sign.

Just then Nurse Anat passed by. "Go in! Go in!" she urged with a smile. "You won't believe what's going on in there!"

Somewhat confused, the two walked right into the middle of an emotional family reunion.

"Oh, look who's here!" cried Uri at the sight of his friends. "*Ima*, here are Moshe and Benny!"

"Come in, boys," Mrs. Segev welcomed them with a smile. "I've heard so many nice things about you."

"Thank you," they murmured politely.

"*Baruch rofei cholim*," said Moshe, at the sight of Uri sitting in a chair. "Blessed is *Hashem*, Who heals the sick."

"May *Hashem* give Mr. Segev and Uri a speedy and complete recovery," said Benny.

"Amen!" said Mrs. Segev, pleased with the blessings. "Please sit down."

Benny and Moshe sat beside Daniel and spoke quietly. They did not want to disturb the family celebration.

Finally, when everyone left the room, the friends gathered around Uri's bed and looked at the pile of gifts his mother had brought him.

"How's your father?" asked Benny.

"He feels much better," said Uri.

"That's wonderful," Daniel quickly put in.

"But he still has a long period of rehabilitation ahead before he will be able to walk again. Because of that," said Uri, looking at his new friends, "we will have to live in the United States for a while."

"What!" exclaimed the friends together. "You're moving to the United States?"

"Only temporarily," said Uri. "Only until my father recovers completely. Then we'll come back, of course." He paused a second and added, "With G-d's help."

"We'll miss you," said Moshe and Benny.

"Uri," said Daniel, "may we be reunited, healthy and well, in the Land of Israel!"

"Amen!" said the others.

Daniel's blessing was to come true in a way he never dreamed possible.

THE CARPET SALESMAN

"Let's sum up what we know so far," said Mr. Berger.

Daniel began. "The main suspect is Jerry Thompson, who lives at 37 Kinor Street."

"Good," said Mr. Berger. "What else?"

"This suspect," Uri picked up the story, "is tracking what is happening in the Defense Department complex on Melech Street."

"Just a minute," Mr. Berger interrupted. "Is he looking for information about the Defense Department itself, or about one of its workers?"

"Why do you ask?" wondered Benny.

"The suspect sits facing the Defense Department complex every day," said Mr. Berger. "Yet he photographs only the black limousine."

Moshe did not follow Mr. Berger's train of thought. "What are you getting at?" he asked.

"He means," explained Daniel, "that Thompson may be trailing the owner of the black limousine."

"How can we find out who the owner is?" asked Moshe.

"We can't," said Benny. "The place is well guarded. You can't just go in and ask whether someone there owns a black limousine."

"Maybe we can," said Mr. Berger thoughtfully. "Maybe we can."

The man who received the photographs knew exactly what to do.

He put them carefully in his shirt pocket, got into his car, and drove to the Old City. He parked the car, got out, and walked quickly through the alleys of the Armenian Quarter. It was obvious that he knew the place well.

Indeed, it was not the first time he needed the services of Ibrahim the carpet merchant.

Ibrahim's carpet shop was nestled in a narrow, filthy alley. Colorful, dusty carpets hung at the entrance of the shop, but even the shopkeeper himself could not remember when he had last sold a carpet.

The man with the photographs went through the arched doorway. He found himself in a room with thick walls and a high ceiling that looked as if it had been standing, unchanged, for centuries. In the middle of the room, amidst piles of rolled-up carpets, Ibrahim sat on a low stool lazily smoking a nargileh.

Now Ibrahim hung the mouthpiece of the nargileh in its place, stood up, and motioned to the customer to follow him.

They walked to the back of the shop. Ibrahim pulled aside a large carpet that was hanging on the wall. Behind it was a modern steel door. Ibrahim pressed some numbers on a small electronic keypad, and the door opened with a hum.

Ibrahim and his customer walked through the door into a modern office that contrasted sharply with the ancient carpet

Ibrahim

shop. The office contained two sophisticated computers, copying machines, a table and chairs, and various tools that served Ibrahim in his main occupation: forging documents.

※◇※

"Have a seat," said Ibrahim. "Now tell me, what document do you need? Israeli identification certificate? American visa? Swiss passport? Just say and pay."

"Not this time," the man replied. "Now I've come to you for a different reason."

Ibrahim listened with interest.

"One of my clients suspects he is being followed. He managed to photograph the follower. I need the follower's identity."

"Is the picture clear?" asked Ibrahim.

"Very." The man placed the photographs on the table.

Ibrahim looked at them thoughtfully. "It will cost you $500," he said at last. "Payment in cash, now."

"Five hundred dollars?" gasped the man in astonishment. "Last time I paid you 200!"

"Five hundred dollars, and not one penny less," Ibrahim repeated without blinking. "If you don't like the price, feel free to take your business elsewhere."

"Okay," sighed the man, his back against the wall. "When will I get an answer?"

"Perhaps tomorrow," replied Ibrahim. "I'll call you the minute I know."

The man put a bundle of bills on the table and left.

Ibrahim took the photographs, sat down at the computer, and got to work.

THE DEFENSE DEPARTMENT COMPLEX

*E*arly in the afternoon, Moshe and Benny went for a stroll with Mr. Berger. They stopped at a small kiosk that offered a tempting selection of candies and snacks.

Mr. Berger treated his young cohorts to ice cream cones. He also bought a bar of fine nut-filled Swiss chocolate, which he put in his pocket.

"Do you like chocolate?" asked Moshe in surprise.

"I used to, when I was younger," replied Mr. Berger. "Now my health does not permit me to eat sweets."

"Then why did you buy a chocolate bar?" asked Benny.

"You will see," said Mr. Berger. "You will see."

After a short walk, the three reached Melech Street and headed toward the Defense Department complex.

Beside the electric gate stood a young soldier with a sub-machine gun slung over his shoulder. He had a pleasant face, and he smiled at them when their eyes met.

"Shalom, young man," Mr. Berger opened the conversation.

"Shalom to you," replied the soldier. "Are these your grandchildren?"

"Sweet, aren't they?" said Mr. Berger. "Please meet Moshe and Benny."

"Did you notice," Benny whispered to Moshe, "how careful Mr. Berger was not to lie? He never said we were his grandchildren!"

"Sh!" said Moshe. "Let me listen to the conversation."

"Pleased to meet you," said the soldier, extending his hand. "I'm Ido."

Mr. Berger put his hand inside his jacket pocket, took out the chocolate bar, and handed it to the soldier.

"Oh, thank you," said Ido in surprise.

"This is only a small token of my gratitude," said Mr. Berger. "You soldiers serve our people so devotedly, guarding our country night and day, winter and summer."

"Just doing my duty," said Ido, embarrassed by the rain of compliments.

"Tell me, Ido," said Mr. Berger, "what are you guarding here so carefully? One would think you have stockpiles of missiles or secret weapons in there."

Ido laughed. "Oh, no. The army never puts such things in the center of a town. But we have things here that are no less important."

"What, for instance?" asked Mr. Berger.

"I'm not allowed to say much," replied Ido. "I can only tell you that there's a research department here that develops sophisticated new weapons."

"Is there any chance," Mr. Berger dared to ask, "that the children could see a little of what goes on inside?"

"No," replied Ido. "No one may enter without a clearly defined purpose."

Suddenly Benny began to tug at Mr. Berger's sleeve. When he caught Mr. Berger's attention, Benny whispered something in his ear.

"Benny would like to know," said Mr. Berger apologetically, "whether there are bathrooms here."

Ido thought for a minute.

"You know what?" he said. "I'll escort you in. The soldier in the guardhouse will cover for me."

Ido exchanged a few words with the other soldier. Then he unlocked a side door. "Follow me," he told them as he went in.

Mr. Berger and the boys looked around carefully and tried to commit every detail to memory.

A number of cars were parked in the big parking lot. Moshe dug his elbow into Benny's ribs and then pulled gently on Mr. Berger's jacket. The two understood the hint.

"Who parks here?" Benny asked Ido.

"Only the staff," Ido replied. "Ordinary soldiers park in the lot across the street."

"Which car belongs to the person in charge?" asked Benny.

"The chief doesn't park in the lot. He has his own special space." Ido pointed to a small, covered space next to a three-story building.

Only one car was parked there.

It was the black limousine.

The Name on the Door

*I*brahim the forger sat in his office behind the carpet shop. On the computer screen before him, pictures appeared one after another in rapid succession. From time to time he would stop the flow of pictures, examine one closely, and save it in a separate file.

Finally, Ibrahim printed out three hundred pictures of old men with short beards and glasses. Then he took a magnifying glass and began to study the pictures carefully, comparing the printouts with the photographs he had been given.

After working for hours, he put down the stack of pages on the table, circled one of the pictures, and said, "Here you are!"

"Write it down," said Ibrahim. "The old man in the picture is Zalman Berger. He lives at 6 Lev Street in Jerusalem."

"I knew I could rely on you," said the man on the other end of the line.

"Thanks," replied Ibrahim. "At your service always."

Ido said to his three new friends, "We will enter the building from here. The bathrooms are at the end of the corridor."

"What is this building used for?" Moshe asked Ido while they waited for Benny.

"This is where the weapons research and development goes on," said Ido. "The chief himself is one of the top researchers and inventors."

"Where does he sit?" asked Moshe. "Does he have his own room?"

"Room?" Ido laughed. "He has a whole big office. It's over there." Ido pointed to a door in the middle of the corridor.

"But the door is closed," said Moshe innocently.

"Indeed," said Ido. "In order to see him, you have to pass three secretaries and one assistant. Only after that can you meet with him, if he is willing to see you."

Benny rejoined them, and they began to walk out. When they passed the chief's office, Moshe stopped for a second. Then he turned white.

"Moshe! What happened?" asked Mr. Berger. "Are you okay?"

"Should I get you some water?" Ido asked in alarm.

Moshe nodded, and Ido hurried to bring him a cup of water.

"What happened?" asked Benny. "Did something frighten you?"

Moshe pointed weakly to the door of the chief's office.

Mr. Berger and Benny approached the door. Beside it was a small sign that read: "Colonel Dr. Gidon Argov."

THE FRIEND

*B*ack in room 210, the group huddled together in conference.

"The picture is becoming clear," said Uri. "Jerry Thompson is shadowing a senior officer in the Defense Department."

"But what can Thompson find out about Colonel Gidon Argov?" said Mr. Berger thoughtfully. "He's so closely guarded!"

"Maybe we should try to get another message from the blind beggar," suggested Moshe.

"You mean from Thompson," Benny corrected him.

"No way," said Mr. Berger firmly. "It's too dangerous."

"So what should we do?" asked Moshe.

The question was left hanging for some time.

"Do you know what we haven't done yet?" Daniel suddenly asked.

Everyone looked at Daniel.

"We haven't found out about the man in the dark hat," Daniel continued.

"Daniel's right," said Uri. "The man in the dark hat is the one who receives the information. If we knew what he did with it, the whole mystery would be solved."

"So our next step," added Moshe, "is to tail the man in the dark hat."

"Let's go right now," said Benny.

The Friend

Mr. Berger glanced at his watch. "It's too late. But tomorrow—tomorrow, *b'ezras Hashem*, we will tail the gentleman in the dark hat."

A dusty brown truck made its way up Lev Street. Big letters on its side proclaimed loudly that the truck's owner bought and sold used furniture.

But the man sitting at the wheel had never dealt in used furniture. He was known as The Friend. No one knew his name or address. People who needed his shady services reached him by calling a certain telephone number and leaving a message.

Upon reaching 6 Lev Street, The Friend parked his truck and got out. His dusty grey overalls fit in with the description of his business. The visor of his cap and a pair of dark sunglasses hid his face.

An old man came out of the small apartment building that bore the sign "6 Lev Street."

"Excuse me," said The Friend, holding a wrinkled piece of paper in his hand. "Do you know a man here by the name of Zalman Berger? Someone told me he's interested in selling an old sofa."

"Of course I know him," came the enthusiastic response. "We've been good neighbors for the past thirty-three years!"

"Very nice," said The Friend, smiling to himself. "What floor does he live on?"

"Zalman lives on the second floor," said the neighbor. Then he added, "But he's usually not at home at this hour."

"He isn't home?" The Friend's face turned serious. "Where is he? At work?"

"No, Zalman retired. But now he volunteers at the hospital every day and he spends most of the day there," the neighbor replied. "But I heard from Mrs. Blumenkrantz, who heard from Mr. Mermelstein, that Zalman will be taking some time off soon, *b'ezras Hashem*. We're looking forward to seeing him around here more often."

"Do you know what hospital he volunteers in?" asked The Friend.

"Of course I know," the neighbor replied.

"So where is he?" asked The Friend, his patience wearing thin.

"Bikurim Hospital," said the neighbor.

"Thank you," said The Friend. He got into the dusty truck and drove off.

In room 210, the countdown began.

"Are you ready, my young sleuths?" Mr. Berger asked Moshe and Benny.

"Ready!" the two answered together.

"Let's go, then," said Mr. Berger. "It's 5 to 6."

A car pulled up at the entrance of the hospital. Out stepped an elegantly dressed man in a well-tailored coat. Today, as every day, he wore dark glasses.

No one would have identified him as the used furniture dealer in dusty grey overalls.

At the entrance to the hospital was a small stand where flowers were sold.

The man stopped at the stand and bought a large bouquet. It will help me hide my face, thought The Friend.

Then he walked into the hospital.

WHO'S FOLLOWING WHOM?

*C*arrying the bouquet before him, the Friend turned toward the elevators.

A number of people were standing around waiting for an elevator to come down. Some were impatient, others bored, still others calm and patient. Some were worried about dear ones who were sick. Others were happy about the birth of a new baby.

A buzz announced the arrival of an elevator. The people waiting to go up moved aside, making way for the passengers to step out of the elevator.

Among the passengers who stepped out of the elevator was Mr. Berger, accompanied by Moshe and Benny.

The Friend, who had spent hours studying Mr. Berger's photographs, recognized the old man immediately. He quickly put the big bouquet of flowers directly in front of his face.

The three walked right by him without suspecting a thing.

He waited for them to move toward the entrance of the hospital. Then he tossed the bouquet into the nearest wastebasket and went out after them.

"Look outside," Mr. Berger whispered to his young escorts. "There's the gentleman in the dark hat. He's preparing to leave. He must have already picked up the envelope that Thompson hid for him. After him, boys!"

Aha! The Friend noted with satisfaction. Here's the old man, with two boys accompanying him. Now everything is clear. They're the ones who took the letter! I must find out who the old man is working for. This calls for an interrogation.

The Friend pulled a tiny but powerful walkie-talkie out of his coat pocket and whispered a few words.

When he was convinced that the man on the other end understood what he had to do, The Friend returned the walkie-talkie to his pocket.

The man in the dark hat would have been surprised by what was taking place behind his back. He was unaware that he was being followed, and that his followers, too, were being followed.

"Tell me, Mr. Berger," asked Moshe. "What will we do if he gets into his car?"

"Don't worry," said Mr. Berger. "There are many taxis around. Have you forgotten Avshalom the driver? We may not find such an expert this time, but we will certainly be able to follow the white car."

"There it is!" said Moshe excitedly.

"There is what?" asked Mr. Berger and Benny together.

"The white car," said Moshe. "Look, over there—a white Mitsubishi with license plate number 765-438-03!"

"Well done," said Benny.

Mr. Berger flagged a taxi.

A van screeched to a halt beside them. The door opened and two men jumped out. Before Mr. Berger, Moshe, and Benny understood what was happening, they were whisked into the van and seated forcibly in the back.

"Don't dare to move," one of the men warned. "And don't get any ideas."

Another person got in and sat in front of them.

It was The Friend.

The van sped ahead.

"Blindfold them," The Friend ordered one of the men. "I don't want them to see anything."

"Anyway there are no windows," said the man.

"Don't argue with me," hissed The Friend. "Blindfold them!"

The Friend turned around and looked at his three captives.

"So you're Zalman Berger," said The Friend, half asking, half asserting.

"I don't recall having made your acquaintance," replied Mr. Berger bravely. "Please remind me, where have we met?"

"We have never met," replied The Friend. "But you are holding in your possession something that belongs to me, something in which I am keenly interested."

"I have something of yours?" Mr. Berger opened his mouth in surprise. "What are you referring to?"

"I'm referring to the envelope," said The Friend. He lowered his voice menacingly. "Where's the envelope?"

"You mean an envelope with money?" asked Mr. Berger innocently. "Are you trying to rob me? My wallet is in the pocket of my jacket."

The Friend got angry. "Don't pretend you don't know," he hissed. "I'm looking for the envelope that you took from the bench in front of the hospital."

"What envelope?" asked Mr. Berger innocently. "I have no idea what you're talking about."

"Fine," muttered The Friend. "When I get finished interrogating you, you'll reveal everything you know. That's a promise."

"I know nothing about any envelope," Mr. Berger insisted. "Absolutely nothing! You have made an unfortunate mistake. I was strolling with my two grandsons, then suddenly we were pulled into this van, and now you ask me questions about envelopes. Let us out, immediately!"

"You aren't as innocent as you pretend to be," said The Friend. "I will hold you and your grandsons until you reveal everything!"

After a 20-minute ride, the van stopped. One of the men got out and opened a rusty iron gate, and the vehicle entered a yard.

"See whether anyone is around," The Friend ordered.

"The coast is clear," said the man who opened the gate.

The three were taken out in blindfolds, brought inside, and led to one of the rooms.

"Now you may remove the blindfolds," said The Friend.

Mr. Berger, Moshe, and Benny did as ordered.

It was a large, empty room. Aside from one old bed in a corner, there was a small, dusty window covered with thick bars.

"You can rot here without food or water until you decide to tell me everything," said The Friend. "When you're ready to talk, knock on the door and I'll come."

The Friend left the room and locked the door behind him.

Mr. Berger put his finger to his lips to keep the boys quiet. He pressed his ear against the door and listened carefully.

Moshe trembled.

"There's nothing to worry about," said Mr. Berger soothingly. "If you don't come home on time, your parents will immediately call Daniel at the hospital and ask where you are. Daniel will tell them what he knows, and your parents will go straight to the police."

"What if the police don't find us?" wailed Moshe.

"Of course they'll find us," said Mr. Berger. "No doubt about it."

Mr. Berger himself didn't believe a word of what he had just said.

In the Locked Room

𝒯he door of the house slammed shut.

Mr. Berger pricked up his ears.

He heard car doors being slammed, then the roar of a car engine coming to life.

"They've left," said Mr. Berger. "Probably went to buy themselves food for supper. They'll be back soon. We'll have to hurry."

"Where can we hurry to in a locked room that we can't get out of?" wondered Benny.

"With help from *Hashem* and a little patience," said Mr. Berger, "we should be able to get out of here."

"Get out of here?" echoed the boys.

"Yes, indeed," Mr. Berger assured them. "Now empty your pockets. Let's see what you have that can help us get out."

The boys emptied their pockets onto the old bed, and Mr. Berger did the same.

A small pile of assorted articles accumulated in the middle of the bed. There was a spool of thread, a key chain, a rubber ball, four rubber bands, a small *siddur*, a wallet, some paper clips, a magnifying glass, a chocolate bar, a snail, reading glasses, a folded newspaper, two pebbles, and a piece of bent wire.

Moshe surveyed the pile with disappointment. "Is that all? Can you explain to me how a magnifying glass will help us get out of here? Will looking at the bars through it make the space between them larger?"

But Mr. Berger beamed with delight. "You don't know what a treasure we have here!"

"Treasure?" echoed the boys. "What treasure?"

"The wire," said Mr. Berger. "It's a treasure!"

"Some treasure," sighed Moshe. "Do you know how many of those we have in the yard behind our house?"

"Do you remember that when they locked the door, I asked you to be quiet?" asked Mr. Berger.

"Yes," said Benny. "And you pressed your ear to the door."

"Correct," said Mr. Berger. "I wanted to hear if they took the key out of the lock."

"Did they take it out?" asked Moshe.

"No," said Mr. Berger. "The key is still in the lock."

"Then we don't stand a chance," said Benny grimly. "As long as the key is in the lock, there's no way to unlock the door from our side."

"You're wrong, my dear boy," said Mr. Berger, "as you'll soon see."

The boys watched in fascination as Mr. Berger spread the newspaper on the floor. Very carefully, he pushed it through the crack between the door and the floor until most of it was outside the room.

When the newspaper was in place, Mr. Berger straightened the wire. He pushed one end of the wire through the keyhole and jiggled it around.

The room was filled with tension. The boys hardly dared breathe.

At last, a metallic ring was heard.

A huge smile lit up Mr. Berger's face. He carefully pulled the newspaper into the room. When it slid inside, on it sat— the key!

"*Baruch Hashem!*" exclaimed Mr. Berger.

"Mr. Berger," cried Moshe, "you're a genius! How do you know all these things?"

The old man smiled modestly. "Oh, it's just an old trick.

"Now," he said gravely, "we must get out of here fast! Our captors are liable to return at any minute!"

Mr. Berger opened the door, and the three went out of the room.

THE SECRET DRAWER

"Okay, we got out of the room," said Moshe, "but how will we get out of the house? When the men left, they surely locked the door behind them!"

"That won't be a problem," said Benny. "Look, we're on the ground floor of a private house. We can climb out of a window."

Benny peeked behind a dusty drape. He peered carefully out the large window.

Something looked familiar.

"Mr. Berger, Moshe," Benny called softly, "do you know where we are?"

"How should we know?" asked Moshe. "We were brought here blindfolded!"

"Come see for yourself," said Benny. "Look." He pointed across the street. "Doesn't that playground look familiar?"

"Sure does," said Moshe. "That's the playground on Kinor Street. We're in Jerry Thompson's house!"

"Nothing could be better!" said Benny. "Let's search the house. If we find real evidence, the police will finally take us seriously. They'll put the gang in jail and foil their wicked plot!"

"That's very noble of you," said Moshe. "But we'd better escape before it's too late. If they come back and find us here, they'll lock us up again—but this time they won't leave us unguarded!"

"Which should we do?" Benny asked Mr. Berger. "Search the house or escape?"

"I think we can do both," said Mr. Berger. "Let's prepare an escape route, so that if they come back we can slip out quickly. Then we'll make a quick search. Does everyone agree?"

"Yes," said Benny and Moshe together.

"The house is almost empty," added Mr. Berger. "The search won't take long."

They found the back door, unlocked it, and peeked out into the backyard. "This is our safety hatch," said Mr. Berger.

Moshe was stationed at the front window as a lookout. "If you see a vehicle pulling up," said Mr. Berger, "call us and we'll all run out the back door."

Moshe was scared. He hoped the others didn't hear his heart, which was beating like a drum.

They started in the living room. Mr. Berger picked up the cushions of the couch. Then he felt them to check whether anything was hidden inside. Benny looked behind all the dusty old pictures hanging on the walls.

They found nothing.

Mr. Berger went on into the kitchen, while Benny stayed to examine an ancient desk in the corner.

Mr. Berger opened the door of the refrigerator and wrinkled his nose in disgust. It had not been cleaned in a long time.

The refrigerator was almost empty. Mr. Berger checked the contents of a few open cans.

"Mr. Berger," called Benny quietly, "please come quickly."

Mr. Berger found Benny standing in the corner facing the antique desk. Its door and three of its drawers were open. They contained papers, pens, and other ordinary articles.

The bottom drawer was closed.

"Look," said Benny. "This drawer is closed even though it has no keyhole. It seems to be stuck. Can you help me open it?"

"Let me take a look," said Mr. Berger.

The old man bent over and examined the drawer carefully. He tapped its sides and gently felt all around it.

"This is what we we've been searching for!" said Mr. Berger decisively. "It's a secret drawer! We have to find the button or lever that opens it."

"That could take hours," Benny objected. "Why don't we just break it open?"

"Not a chance," said Mr. Berger. "My guess it that this drawer is a small safe. It's unbreakable and even fireproof."

"So what shall we do?" asked Benny.

"Let's search the room for a button or lever," said Mr. Berger.

Benny walked slowly around the living room, feeling the smooth walls with his hands. Mr. Berger sat on a chair in the middle of the room, carefully surveying every detail.

"Use your head!" Mr. Berger muttered to himself. "Use your head!"

The search turned up nothing.

"Let's leave," said Mr. Berger. "It's getting late, and our captors are liable to return at any minute."

The three hurried toward the back door. On the way, they passed a dusty shelf that proudly displayed an ivory horse, a miniature Eiffel Tower, and an old picture in an ornate frame. In his haste to escape, Moshe accidentally knocked over the miniature Eiffel Tower.

A sharp click was immediately heard. They all stopped dead in their tracks and looked around the room.

The bottom drawer of the antique desk had flown open.

"I don't believe it," said Benny. "Moshe, you opened the drawer!"

"Benny," said Mr. Berger, "go stand guard at the window. Moshe and I are going to see what's in that drawer!"

THE CIGARETTE LIGHTER

*I*n sharp contrast to the rest of the house, the drawer was neat and clean. Inside was a closed folder, a pile of papers covered with a close-written scrawl, and a small box.

Mr. Berger opened the box and looked at it. Then he handed it silently to Moshe.

"A silver cigarette lighter!" exclaimed Moshe. "Do you think it's the one we saw Thompson use to photograph the black limousine?"

"If it is, there will be a miniature camera inside," said Mr. Berger. "But we have no time to check now. Let's just take everything and leave."

He covered the box carefully to protect the lighter, scooped up the contents of the drawer, and turned to leave.

Moshe pushed the drawer in. It clicked shut.

Just then Benny ran over, pale as a ghost.

"They're coming," he whispered in fright.

"Run to the back door!" said Mr. Berger. "Quickly!"

The three ran out the back door.

The backyard of Thompson's house was surrounded by a tall fence that separated it from the neighbors' yards.

The boys could climb the fence. But what about the old man?

"Run!" said Mr. Berger. "Don't wait for me. We'll meet in room 210!"

"No," said Moshe. "We won't leave you here!"

"Look!" said Benny, pointing. "There's a hole in the fence. It's big enough to climb through!"

The three hurried through the hole in the fence and into a neighboring yard. From there, they went around the side of the neighboring house and looked cautiously out to the street.

"The coast is clear," said Mr. Berger. "Let's go!"

They ran out into the quiet street.

Just then, a taxi stopped to let out a mother holding a sleeping baby. Before the driver understood what was happening, Mr. Berger, Moshe, and Benny were seated in the back.

The driver looked at them in his rear-view mirror. "Did you just come out of a cave?" he asked.

"Cave?" asked the passengers in surprise. "What do you mean?"

"You're covered with dust," said the taxi driver. "Well, where do you want to go?"

"To the central police station," said Mr. Berger. "We have to meet someone there."

"In my opinion," muttered the taxi driver, "you should meet a bathtub!"

"Do you think they know we escaped?" whispered Benny.

"For sure," Mr. Berger whispered back. "They can't miss the open drawer."

"I closed the drawer before we left," said Moshe.

"Wonderful, Moshe!" said Mr. Berger. "If so, they won't know we escaped—at least not till they decide to go into our room or to take something from the drawer.

"Let's hope they don't know yet. That way, the police will be able to capture the whole gang at once."

In the Police Station

An old man and two boys covered with dust appeared at the central police station. They demanded to meet with the chief of police immediately and refused to take no for an answer.

The policewoman on duty tried to convince them to meet first with a policeman of lower rank, but to no avail. The three insisted that it was a case of espionage and time was of the essence.

Ridiculous, thought the policewoman. Nevertheless, just in case there was any truth to their strange claims, she called her superior.

Chief of Police Yossi Stern happened to be there at the time. He overheard the conversation, and his curiosity was piqued. He decided to take a few minutes from his busy schedule to meet with the strange group.

The three were shown into Stern's office. The old man quickly told his story. As Stern listened, the expression on his face turned from one of mild amusement to tense interest.

"Attention all police cars!" he roared into his walkie-talkie. "All police cars to 37 Kinor Street. Arrest everyone in the house immediately. Be careful! The suspects are dangerous and may be armed."

The message was picked up by police cars all over

Jerusalem. With sirens screeching and lights flashing, dozens of police cars sped to Kinor Street.

"Come with me," Stern told Mr. Berger, Moshe, and Benny. "Let's go to the scene of the action."

All four piled into Stern's car. It took off with a screech of tires.

"Shlomo! Look what's going on right here on our block!" Mrs. Brook shook the shoulder of her husband, who was dozing over the newspaper. "It's full of police cars. Looks like they're arresting someone."

"We've been living on Kinor Street for thirty years already," said Mr. Brook. "Never have I seen a single police car here."

"Then you won't want to miss this," said his wife. "Hurry to the window!"

Scores of policemen took up positions around the house. Two kicked the door open, and ten burst inside.

The three gang members were quietly eating supper. They were too surprised to put up any resistance.

The policemen put chains on the suspects' hands and feet and led them into a closed police van.

The suspects would finish their supper in jail.

The following day a press conference was held.

"Mr. Chief of Police," said an excited reporter, "is it true that last night you arrested members of a dangerous gang?"

"I am not at liberty to give out details yet," said Stern. "But I will tell you this: Additional arrests are now being made on the basis of the investigation of the suspects arrested yesterday."

"Can you tell us what led to the discovery of the gang?" asked another reporter.

"The question is not what led to the discovery," said Stern, "but who led to it. The people who solved this case have asked to remain anonymous, and I must respect their wishes. But I can say that all of us owe a tremendous debt of gratitude to a few civilians—some of whom are quite young. These noble souls acted with courage, resourcefulness, and wisdom to protect us all."

A Meeting in Room 210

*C*hief of Police Yossi Stern arrived in room 210 with another three senior officers. Colonel Gidon Argov arrived with his wife. The mayor showed up a few minutes later. Velvel Weinstein was already there, as were Uri's mother and the parents of Moshe, Benny, and Daniel.

An officer closed the door to room 210, and the chief of police addressed the assembled.

"Ladies and gentlemen, we have gathered here this evening to thank our brave heroes—Mr. Berger, Moshe, Benny, Daniel, and Uri—for their amazing contribution to the safety of our citizens.

"On this happy occasion, I would like to update you concerning the investigation. Many details must still remain top secret for reasons of national security. But I will tell you as much as I can.

"Our group of sleuths here have exposed one of the most dangerous espionage rings ever to operate in the State of Israel. The ring included senior spies who infiltrated our weapons research and development program.

"Moreover, they planned to kidnap one of the senior commanders and scientists in that program—Colonel Gidon Argov, who is here with us now—and hold him in enemy territory.

"This plan was to be carried out within the next few days. Our sleuths exposed the ring and foiled their scheme in the nick of time.

"And that's not all.

"Among the suspects arrested was a scoundrel known as The Friend. For years, we have been trying to lay our hands on The Friend and put him behind bars, but he always managed to evade the hands of the law. With The Friend in prison, many people will be able to sleep safely at night.

"You may be wondering how I can be sure that the courts will convict these suspects and put them in prison.

"The answer is that we have proof! Mr. Berger, Moshe, and Benny found invaluable secret documents. They also found a tiny camera hidden inside an ordinary cigarette lighter.

"Our laboratory developed the film in the camera. The top brass of the Defense Department could not believe their eyes when they saw the photographs.

"To conclude," said the chief of police, "I would like to thank you—Mr. Berger, Moshe, Benny, Daniel, and Uri—on behalf of the entire Police Department. And as a small token of gratitude, I would like to invite the five of you for a trip in a police helicopter, as soon as Daniel and Uri are up to it."

THE CHAVRUSA

Seven years later.

𝒯he bus stopped at the bottom of the hill, opened its doors, and discharged a passenger.

The teenager paused for a moment and looked up at Yeshivah Toras Chaim, set proudly on the hilltop. Then he swung the straps of the duffle bag over his shoulder and walked quickly up the hill.

He entered the building.

"*Shalom aleichem*," one of the students greeted him warmly. "Are you the new student? We're expecting you. Please put your bag down here. My name is Yechezkel Brown—Chezky for short," he added with a smile.

"Pleased to meet you," the newcomer answered shyly. "I'm Daniel Green. Can you tell me where to go?"

"First," said Chezky, "let's go to the office to register. Then you'll get a room and put your things away."

Daniel was grateful to Chezky for the gracious reception. When you come to a new place, a friendly greeting makes all the difference in the world.

The room to which Daniel was assigned was large and neat. His roommates welcomed him and helped him get settled. Then Daniel headed for the *beis midrash*.

Over one hundred students were studying loudly and enthusiastically. Some looked intently at the *Gemara* in front of them, while others hotly debated its meaning with their friends.

"Now," said Chezky, "all I have to do is arrange a suitable *chavrusa* for you to study with."

"How will I find a *chavrusa*?" asked Daniel. "I don't know anyone here!"

"Nachman is in charge of arranging *chavrusos*," said Chezky. "Come, I'll introduce you."

"So you're Daniel Green," said Nachman. "The Rosh Yeshivah was very impressed with your answers when he tested you. He told me that an excellent new student was coming here."

Daniel blushed.

"That is why," said Nachman, getting down to business, "I've arranged for your *chavrusa* to be one of the yeshivah's best students!"

Nachman pointed to a teenager who was sitting beside an open *Gemara* with his back toward them. He was swaying back and forth enthusiastically.

"Go over to him," said Nachman, "and tell him Nachman sent you."

"What's his name?" asked Daniel.

"Oh, did I forget to tell you?" asked Nachman. "His name is Uri Segev."